6X

PAINTED LADY

Felicity Grant is Managing Director of Grant Holdings, and with Stallymore Castle as her headquarters and home, she's used to being sure of every decision she makes. She commissions Jake Ashton to paint a portrait of the Board, but for no reason she can fathom, he gets under her skin in a way no one else has.

Then her father is taken ill, at the same time as news breaks of a spy in Grant Holdings. Felicity's place as MD is in doubt – can she regain the trust of the Board whilst discovering who is determined to take over her position?

PAINTED LADY

PAINTED LADY

by

Donna Baker

Magna Large Print Books
Long Preston, North Yorkshire,
BD23 4ND, England.

British Library Cataloguing in Publication Data.

Baker, Donna
  Painted lady.

  A catalogue record of this book is
  available from the British Library

  ISBN   0-7505-1603-8

First published in Great Britain 2000 by
Severn House Publishers Ltd.

Published in Large Print 2001 by arrangement with
Severn House Publishers Ltd.

Magna Large Print is an imprint of Library Magna Books Ltd.

Printed and bound in Great Britain by
T.J. (International) Ltd., Cornwall, PL28 8RW

One

On the day that Felicity met Jake Ashton, she was feeling at her best. Cool, crisp, assertive, successful – a woman of 2000, at the head of a thriving business with even greater triumphs before her. Not the kind of woman to be caught by the trap of romance.

Not that the possibility had never arisen. At twenty-seven, with an effortlessly slim figure, shining ebony hair and wide grey eyes, Felicity had attracted a good many men, but none of them had been able to offer anything to match what she already had. Life was too exciting as it was – and she took a delighted pride in seeing what she had achieved entirely alone.

There were men on her board, naturally, but not – she often thought with a quirk of her lips – in her bed. And that was the way she wanted it to stay.

'Mr Ashton to see you, Miss Grant.'

Felicity, sitting behind her desk in the large, oak-panelled room she had chosen as her office, gave a little jump, surprised to find that her thoughts had been straying from the papers on her desk. She glanced up at her secretary and gave a little nod.

'Show him in, please, Jackie.'

The door opened a little wider, and Felicity watched with interest. The man who was about to come in wasn't the kind of person she normally associated with. Her life was spent with businessmen: accountants, salesmen, directors who held degrees in such subjects as law or economics, men who were sophisticated enough to take air travel, high-powered cars and luxury hotels for granted. An artist was quite outside her experience and she wasn't quite sure what to expect.

'Mr Ashton.'

Jackie withdrew and Felicity sat quite still for a moment, her eyes widening as they took in the man before her. Then, slowly, she stood up and walked round the desk, extending her hand. As she touched the strong fingers in the handshake that was normally no more than a meaningless formality, her skin tingled.

'Good morning, Mr Ashton. It's very kind of you to come. Please sit down.' Her voice shook a little and she stopped abruptly, annoyed with herself. What on earth was she doing, reacting like this?

Jake Ashton gave her a lazy smile which reached his dark brown eyes, and coiled his long body into one of the armchairs. Felicity took the chair opposite, feeling oddly at a loss. She glanced under her violet-tipped lashes at his clothes – not at all the kind of thing her directors would have worn to visit her. With his open-necked shirt, dark blue trousers, coloured waistcoat and a red scarf knotted loosely round his neck, his thick black hair and short, curling beard, he looked more than a touch unconventional, almost gypsy-like, she thought, and felt a sudden shiver as if she had scented danger.

'Well?' he asked after a moment, in a deep voice that held a tinge of amusement. 'Do I pass muster?'

'I – I beg your pardon?' To her annoyance, she found herself stuttering. What was the *matter* with her, for goodness' sake? She dealt with men every day of the week – men who were accustomed to hard-nosed business deals, who never gave an inch – and none of them had ever affected her like this. It was because he was from a different world, she reminded herself. She needed to find some common ground. Meanwhile, she had plenty of resources at her command.

The best thing was to treat him as she would any other employee.

'I'm sorry,' she said crisply, getting her voice under control again. 'I don't quite understand–'

'You're looking at me as if I'm some creature from another planet,' he said cheerfully, echoing her thoughts with uncanny accuracy, 'as if you expected me to come in wearing gold earrings and playing a violin. Or maybe I should be dressed in an artist's smock with paintbrushes sticking out of the pocket, still wet from the latest masterpiece.'

Felicity opened her mouth but no words came. Damn him, she thought crossly.

'But as you can see, I'm just an ordinary guy,' he went on with a friendly grin. 'I just happen to paint for a living. Like you – er – do whatever it is you do.'

'I'm Chairman and Managing Director of Grant Industrial Holdings,' Felicity said stiffly. 'We have divisions dealing with packaging and printing, construction and builders' merchanting. Stallymore Castle is our headquarters and–'

'Oh, I know all that,' he interrupted. 'But that doesn't tell me what you *do*.' He gazed around the big room, at the thick comfort of the carpet, the huge desk where Felicity

12

worked and the smaller desk in the corner where her secretary worked occasionally. He took in the armchairs where her executives sat for informal meetings, the dark wood of the panelled walls, the huge oil-paintings of stern, bewhiskered gentlemen who had once owned Stallymore Castle, the wide, mullioned windows overlooking the soft Devonshire landscape.

'I happen to be a very busy person,' Felicity said coldly. 'So if you don't mind–'

But Jake Ashton interrupted as if he had not heard her speak. With his eyes still on the windows and their sweeping view of lush, rolling fields, thick green woods and the distant blue hills of Dartmoor, he said softly, 'Don't you ever just want to leave all this – get out there in the fresh air and *walk*, without any idea about where you're going? Just let your feet take you wherever the wind blows: sleep in the heather, drink from a stream and go on again next day, for ever and ever, until at last you find a place you want to stop? Don't you ever get sick and tired of your busy life?'

Felicity stared at him. His words brought an uneasiness she didn't like and which she quickly pushed away. She wondered if this had been such a good idea after all. Why, the

13

man was plain eccentric! Perhaps he did have gypsy blood in him. After all, he looked *right* with the waistcoat and neckerchief, he only needed the earring. She had a swift mental picture of him lounging by a camp fire, leaping up to dance in the flickering shadows, slipping away into the darkness with a soft, panther's tread... Quickly, angrily, she thrust the picture away.

'I do go out, quite often,' she said icily. 'As you may have noticed, a great deal has been done to the grounds here. They've been rescued from the wilderness they were when I bought the castle and restored it to order. But perhaps you didn't know them as they were before – I understand you've only recently come to live locally.'

'Oh, I knew them,' he said. 'I lived here years ago. Yes, you've certainly wrought some changes here.' But he didn't sound as if he particularly liked them. 'And is that the extent of your roaming? In those parts of the grounds that have been – "restored to order"?'

'I don't have time to go any further. As I've already told you, I'm a very–'

'Very busy person,' he finished for her and she flinched at the ironic tone in his voice. 'Well, that being the case then, I'm sure you'd like to get down to business. Though I must admit I'm a little surprised that you've sent for me. I'd have expected you to engage a much more well-known artist for such an important picture.'

Felicity gave him a quick glance, but his expression was as bland as his voice.

'Your name was suggested to the Board by my cousin, Andrew Grant,' she said. 'He's one of our non-executive directors – he inherited the castle from our grandfather and came on the Board when I bought it from him. He said he knew of you and thought you'd do a good job.'

Jake Ashton's eyebrows rose. 'Andrew! I thought he lived abroad.'

'He does, most of the time. He was never really interested in Stallymore and only too pleased that it was staying in the family.'

'Even though it's not a home any more,' Jake said, and once again Felicity was aware of that undercurrent of disapproval.

'Look,' she flashed, 'when I bought Stallymore it was just about falling to pieces. I could have bought a place that needed nothing doing to it – I could have set up my headquarters anywhere. Then what would have happened? The whole place would have deteriorated beyond repair. Andrew would never have rescued it – it was just a millstone round his neck. He was glad to sell it to me, and glad that I've done what I have to it. And for your information, it *is* a home. My home.'

He gave her an oblique glance. 'I'm glad to hear it,' he said politely. 'But I didn't exactly have in mind a luxury suite for the chairman when I referred to a home. I was thinking more of – well, of half a dozen kids, assorted dogs and muddy footprints in the hall. That sort of thing.'

Felicity stared at him and was immediately wafted back twenty years, to the days when she had come to stay here with her grandfather and various aunts, uncles and cousins. The castle had been neglected then but nobody had seemed to care. They'd lived in the few habitable rooms and closed the others off. The Great Hall had been a huge family room, with the big dining table in one corner and a table-tennis table in another, with dogs stretched out in front of the fireplace, cousins sprawled on the old rugs playing Monopoly, Chinese Chequers or Scrabble, the adults settled into shabby sofas and armchairs listening to music on the old record player or talking in lazy, holiday voices. Outside had been the

16

tangled gardens, a child's paradise of overgrown shrubs and bushes which had hidden ponds crowded with waterlilies and jumping with frogs. And beyond those, the woods, cool and dark, with the secret lake...

'Well, it's not like that now,' she said sharply, coming back to the present. She got up and walked with quick, short steps over to the window, staring down at the smooth lawns and orderly borders. The sight gave her a kind of reassurance and she turned to face Jake, once again in command of herself.

'The picture. Have you any idea how long it would take?'

Jake's dark brown eyes flickered for a moment and she reminded herself that this man wasn't an ordinary employee. He was an independent individual, more like a consultant. Though to put him in that class was of course ridiculous. Painting was hardly a real job.

'That depends on how sittings could be arranged,' he answered easily. 'I shall need to see the whole Board, of course, both in whichever setting we decide to use and individually. I shall need to spend some time with each one–'

'Why on earth do you need to do that?'

she broke in.

'So that I can get to know them.' His tone was unperturbed. 'So that I can get an idea of the kind of people they are, see their facial expressions, their mannerisms, what sets them on fire. You want me to do the best by each member of the Board, don't you?' There was just the faintest emphasis on the word 'each' – almost as if he thought her guilty of wanting the portrait to be primarily of herself, with the other members mere background figures.

'Of course I do,' she said quickly. 'But I wouldn't have thought–'

'Let's make a deal,' he said. 'You don't tell me how to paint pictures and I don't tell you how to run a company. OK?' She looked at him and saw he was grinning. For a moment or two, she fought a strong desire to ring for Jackie and ask her to show Mr Ashton out. Then she realised how ridiculous that would be and gave him a small smile in return.

'It's a deal,' she said, and felt the smile widen. He really was rather attractive... Abruptly, she stopped smiling and moved briskly to her desk. 'Now, we'd better get something organised for these sittings. What exactly do you–'

'Don't stop.' He had moved as quickly as she and was standing close beside her as she looked down at her papers. Felicity could feel the warmth of his breath on her cheek and when she turned her head, his face was unnervingly close to hers.

'Stop what?' She took a step away and was immediately annoyed; she shouldn't let him get to her like this. 'I'm sorry, I don't–'

'I meant, don't stop smiling.' He hadn't taken her hint that he was standing too close. 'You've got a lovely smile lurking in there somewhere. Why not let it out occasionally and give us all a treat?'

Felicity stared at him. Her heart was beating fast, her stomach was tingling and there was a strange ache spreading out from somewhere in her breast, down her arms, right into the palms of her hands. She felt a trembling begin deep inside and took another step back. Why did he have to stand so close? Couldn't he see he was crowding her?

'The sittings,' he said gently, as if reminding her, and she turned back in relief to her desk.

'You'll have to discuss that with my secretary – she handles all my appointments.' She bent and flicked the switch on her intercom.

'Jackie? Mr Ashton needs to arrange some appointments for sittings for the Board painting. If you could just have a few dates ready when he comes out? Thanks.' She flicked the switch and turned back to the artist, thankfully noting that he had moved away and was strolling round the room, gazing up at the paintings already on the walls. 'Do we need to discuss anything else?'

'I should think so.' Once again there was that aggravating note of amusement in his voice. 'We've discussed hardly anything so far. I'd like to know several things. First, most important, the setting. Where do you see this portrait actually being executed?'

'In the boardroom, of course. Isn't that the usual thing? With all the members seated round the table in conference.'

'And you at the head. Yes, that's a common way of doing these things.' His voice indicated that he didn't think much of it. 'Have you considered any other options? Something a shade less formal, perhaps?'

'Such as?'

'Well, I haven't seen your boardroom yet, of course, but I'd rather like to use this room. It's such a fine room, such good proportions, and with all this beautiful old panelling–'

'The boardroom has oak panelling too.'

He acknowledged this with a slight movement of his head. 'And there's the view from the window – don't tell me, the boardroom has that too. But most of all, it has this desk and you behind it.' He shot her a swift glance. 'I don't think you realise just how effective you look at your desk, Miss Grant. And how unexpected. With the rest of your Board grouped around, as if you were having a discussion, not to say a thumping good argument, this picture could really come to life. It could be a *picture* – not just a staid representation that could have been posed by a set of dummies.'

Felicity was silent. She couldn't help seeing what he meant. All the same – did she really want that kind of picture? Did the rest of the Board? She knew that when this idea had been first mooted they'd all been envisaging the traditional Board meeting portrayed on canvas. How would they take to the idea of a 'thumping good argument' being captured for posterity?

'Well, think about it,' Jake said. 'Let's see the other rooms we could use, the boardroom and the Great Hall. You use that too, don't you?'

'Yes. It's been restored, just like the rest of

the castle, and furnished as it should be. We use it for special functions – dinners for conferences and so on. That's another reason why I wanted Stallymore, to have somewhere really special as well as spacious and efficient for running training sessions and holding business conferences. We can accommodate up to thirty at a time, so the whole place is well used.' She stopped. 'But you're not interested in that. The Great Hall could be a very good setting, with the table laid for dinner with all the glass and silver and flowers and so on.' The more she thought about it, the more she liked the idea. 'I'll show you now, if you like.'

'Yourself?' he asked. 'Not your secretary?'

Felicity gave him a sharp look, but he was straightfaced. All the same, she thought, he's right. That *is* a job I'd normally ask Jackie to do. And it would make more sense – there was plenty of work waiting on her desk, plus a telephone call or two she needed to make.

'I can spare a few minutes,' she said briefly, and led him out of the office, pausing to let Jackie know where she'd be.

It was pride, of course, she thought as they walked together down the long, curving staircase. Pride in this place and everything she'd done here. A few years ago, this staircase had been dilapidated, the treads threatened by dry rot, the carved banister attacked by woodworm. Now all that had changed; the dry rot had been eradicated and she had found a craftsman who had restored the banister to its former glory. And that was only a tiny part of all that had been achieved.

The Great Hall was the summit of that achievement. As they stood in the doorway, Felicity felt a swell of pleasure. From the glistening chandelier to the enormous picture at one end of Lady Anne Stallymore, who had lived here when the present castle was built, three hundred years ago, the room was exactly right. A showplace.

'Mm,' Jake said when she pointed this out to him. 'Yes, it certainly is. You're to be congratulated, Miss Grant. Only pity is, nobody ever sees it.'

'Nobody sees it!' She stared at him. 'I told you, we use it quite a lot – for entertaining overseas visitors as well as our special functions. It adds a great deal of prestige to the company's image.'

'And that's the main thing, isn't it,' he said ironically. 'Well, I suppose it's no different from what the place has always been used

23

for. What were castles, after all, but a symbol of wealth and power? Image-makers. Frighteners. I just think it's a pity that the only people you show it to are the ones you want to impress, businesswise.'

Felicity felt again that irritating uneasiness. 'Who else should we be showing it to, then?' she asked in a hostile tone.

'Why, anyone who might appreciate it. The local peasants, like me. Holidaymakers – there are plenty about in this area and a lot of them would love to see a place like this. You've got that old keep, all that's left of the original Norman castle – that could be a real feature. The gardens, too, ought to have people walking in them, enjoying the flowers. Enjoying those intriguing woods, as well.' He gave her a sudden, slanting glance. 'I bet there are all kinds of secrets in those woods, don't you, Miss Grant?'

Felicity wanted to turn away, but her eyes were held by his, as dark and secret as a hidden lake. She felt the warm colour mount into her cheeks and knew that he saw it and was amused by it. She felt her heart begin to hammer again, and at last gathered the strength to turn her head.

'There's no question of letting the public in,' she said curtly. 'How could the place function efficiently if there were strangers wandering about all the time? Now, if you've seen enough...?'

'Oh, I think so. I imagine you'll be allowing *me* to wander about, anyway, if you decide to commission the picture.' She turned and gave him a glance of surprise. Although there had been no contract signed, she had assumed that a commission was understood. For a moment she played with the idea of turning him down, telling him that the picture wasn't going to be commissioned after all, telling the Board that she'd decided to try a different artist. Then she thought of how she was to explain her change of mind, what reasons she would have to give, and knew it was impossible. Successful though she was, there were always a few men, even on her own Board, who wouldn't be sorry to see her acting unpredictably, unable to give sound, concrete reasons for her decision. Acting like a woman, in fact.

And that could be the beginning of the end. That could be enough to start the whisper that she wasn't up to the job any more.

No. Andrew had suggested this man and the rest of the Board, having seen some of his work and considered his reputation, had agreed. She would have to go through with it.

'We'll go and see the boardroom now,' she said crisply, and led the way out of the Great Hall, her high heels tapping on the polished wooden floor.

The boardroom was on the less sunny side of the house and even on this warm June morning Felicity found herself shivering a little as she opened the door. Sometimes, as she sat in here chairing an important meeting, she wondered just what had happened in this room in the past to give it such a chill. The thought brought prickles to her spine and she always dismissed it hastily but now, standing here with Jake Ashton at her elbow, she felt it again more strongly than ever.

'My God,' he said in a low voice, and his murmur seemed to reverberate round the silent walls. 'This is a gloomy place. Don't you get spooked in here?'

'Spooked?'

'Get the feeling it's haunted,' he elaborated. 'I can tell you this, I wouldn't want to have to make decisions in here. And I certainly don't want to paint in here.'

Felicity closed the door with some relief, though she didn't intend to let Jake know that she shared his sense of the room being haunted, or that she found the fact that they shared it even more disturbing. 'So it's the Great Hall.'

'Or your office. I still favour that, you know. Not so grand, I admit, but I can paint you a picture there which will throb with vitality. And isn't that the kind of image a go-getting company wants to foster these days?' He went on eagerly as Felicity stopped to look at him. 'Look, boardroom pictures are out, dated. They're too static, there's no life in them. But the picture I've got in mind would show every director as a living person, a strong man in his own right–'

'Two of our members are women,' Felicity interrupted. 'As well as me.'

'All right then, a strong man or woman in his or her own right.' He brushed her interruption aside. 'Sex isn't important – individuality is. And each individual, depicted in that situation, will give a picture of your company as an equally individual and vital entity. Something strong, successful, thrusting. Isn't that the impression you want to give?'

'But this picture will only be for our own walls–'

'Why? Why not use it for something more than that? On your brochures, your annual report? Look, I can paint you a picture that will deserve to be seen – a picture that can say it all for you. And I hope you'll use it, not just hang it on the wall where after a while it will become as invisible as all the rest of those old codgers you've got glowering down from the walls of your office.'

His eyes were alight now, glimmering like the eyes of a tiger as it prowled through the jungle. And Felicity, gazing up into them, felt for a moment that she was the prey the tiger sought. He moved his head slightly; the light changed and once again his eyes were secret, hidden pools. They had tiny flecks of gold in them, she noticed, like a dusting of sunshine filtering down through the shifting branches of the trees. She had a sudden feeling that he was about to reach out and touch her, and she moved abruptly away.

'Well?' he said. 'What do you think?'

'I'll have to talk to the other Board members,' she said, struggling to keep her voice cool. 'I'll let you know. Meanwhile–'

'We'd better fix up some sittings.' He seemed quite cheerful about her withdrawal. 'Shall we go back up and see what your secretary has got lined up?'

They returned to her office in silence. Felicity was still struggling to come to terms with the strange sensations that were playing havoc with the functioning of her heart and lungs. Really, she scolded herself, you're behaving like some demented teenager! So he's different from the men you usually deal with – does that mean you have to go to pieces? You're acting as if you're scared of him, for heaven's sake!

Jackie looked up with a smile as they came back, and picked up a sheet of paper. 'There's a full Board meeting next week, Miss Grant, and another in a fortnight's time. And Mr Andrew will be here during the fortnight, he's staying over, you remember, so I expect some of the others will be calling to see him as well. We should be able to arrange times with them all individually, as Mr Ashton asked.'

'That's fine, Jackie, thank you.' Felicity hesitated. She wanted to say goodbye to Jake Ashton here, in the outer office, and return to her work, but something held her back. Instead of holding out her hand, she heard herself saying, 'Bring some coffee in for us, would you, Jackie? Mr Ashton and I have a few final points to discuss.' And she moved past the secretary's desk into her own light, sunny office.

Once there, she found she didn't know what to say. What was there to discuss, after all? A fee would be negotiated later, a contract drawn up and signed, but all that could be dealt with through the post. She moved to the window and stood tapping her fingertips on the sill, feeling awkward and tongue-tied.

Jake Ashton came to stand beside her. Together, they gazed down at the pleasant gardens, watching Mudge, the gardener, as he moved slowly amongst the roses.

'Imagining it filled with people?' he asked softly. 'Or are you thinking of those kids and dogs and muddy footprints?'

Felicity wheeled to face him.

'Tell me, Mr Ashton. What got you into this? How did you come to be painting pictures of company Boards for a living? I'm sure no boy ever sets out with that as his ambition!'

Jake looked down at her. His face was impassive, but she thought she detected a spark of something – anger? embarrass-ment? – somewhere deep in those eyes, and she felt a little tremor pass across her skin.

'You speak,' he said after a moment, 'as if

it were something to be ashamed of.'

'I didn't say that. I just think–' she paused, choosing her words 'I suppose I just think it doesn't seem much like a real job. A career.' She saw his face darken and hurried on, conscious that she was hitting a nerve but unable to stop. 'I mean, you're not a really creative artist, are you? Painting for the love of it. What you do is solely commercial. You must have had some dream when you began. What happened to it?'

She stopped, aware that her probing had gone too far. Why was she behaving like this, touching on the areas that nobody liked to have exposed: private dreams, secret ambitions? Was it that remark about kids and muddy footprints, with the picture it conjured up of Stallymore Castle as it had once been?

'I'm sorry,' she said quietly. 'I had no right to ask that.'

'It's perfectly all right,' Jake Ashton said. 'I suppose it does seem strange to someone like you. Probably any kind of creativity for its own sake, rather than for commercial gain, would. What surprises me is that you find it odd that I should make money from what talent I have. Even artists have to live, you know.'

'So it's a kind of potboiling.'

'And I didn't say that.' There was a moment of silence before he continued. 'We all have our dreams, Miss Grant. Some of us get to fulfil them. The rest – well, we have to do what we can as well as we can. And this picture – if you still want me to paint it – will be the best I can do. At least, it will be if I'm permitted to do it in the way I want – the way I visualise it. Otherwise – yes, it will be a potboiler, I'm afraid. Static and uninteresting.'

'I've annoyed you,' Felicity said, and looked out of the window again, feeling oddly chilled.

'No. Just displayed to me what a yawning gulf lies between the commercial world and what I consider to be the real world.'

Immediately, she turned on him. 'The real world? But my world is the real world! We live in a commercial world, Mr Ashton – everything revolves around commerce now. Take that away and the world would collapse.'

'Not mine,' he said quietly, and looked down at the gardens. 'All that down there – it didn't collapse before. It wouldn't again. If you went bankrupt tomorrow, Miss Grant, and had to leave the castle, those gardens would still be there, and those woods and hills and moors. Only the disruptive human influence would have gone.'

'Disruptive?' she sneered. 'And what sort of state would they be in inside six months, tell me that. Back to a wilderness, just as they were before.' And a picture flashed into her mind's eye of children, grubby and dishevelled in old clothes, playing in their 'jungle' with a crowd of leaping, lolloping dogs.

'And would that be such a very bad thing?' he asked, and moved away as Jackie came in with the coffee. 'Ah, that smells good.' He gave the secretary a slow, crinkling smile that Felicity could see had her buckling at the knees. 'The first attribute of a first-class secretary – the ability to produce first-class coffee.'

Felicity came over to the low table where Jackie had set the tray. The sooner she poured this out, the sooner she could send Jake Ashton on his way. She groaned silently, remembering that he would be back – again and again. Haunting her office, where he was determined to set this picture of his. Well, she'd see what the Board had to say about that. If they decided the picture must be set in the boardroom or the Great Hall, Jake Ashton would have to go along with their decision, creative impulses or not.

At that moment, she wished heartily that the idea of a picture had never arisen. And especially that her cousin Andrew had never heard of this man, who lived so conveniently locally.

Almost any other artist would have been preferable to him. But why, she found herself thinking, why did she find him so disturbing? It was impossible to say.

Two

'Well, that just about wraps it up. We'll get on to Haverford's first thing Monday morning about the contract, and then things should start moving. I think it's going to be a very successful operation.' Felicity closed the file on her desk and smiled at her companion. 'Thanks to you, Geoff.'

Geoffrey Hall leaned back in his chair and gave a small, dismissive flap of his hand. 'Nonsense. It was a team effort, like everything else here. The whole workforce is behind you to the hilt, Felicity – not to mention the Board. You know that.'

'Mm.' But there was a tiny frown on Felicity's smooth forehead. 'I'm not so sure they all are, Geoff. I've had a feeling lately that there are one or two of our stalwart members who wouldn't be at all grief-stricken to see me go, so that they could step into the chairman's shoes. I may be imagining it–'

'Of course you are!' The pale face opposite flushed with indignation as its owner came upright in his seat. 'If not, they'll have me to deal with. Who are these traitors, anyway?'

Felicity laughed a little. 'I didn't say they were traitors, Geoff. And I'd rather not mention any names. It's just a feeling occasionally, nothing more. And really, wouldn't it be surprising if there weren't one or two with their eyes on their own careers? That's all it is, I'm sure.'

Geoffrey gave her a dubious glance and settled back again. 'Well, if you say so. But I hope you'll trust me, Felicity – at least enough to tell me the moment you have any real suspicion. I won't have anyone dealing behind your back, and I hope they all realise that.'

'It's all right,' Felicity said quietly. 'I'm

quite able to look after myself. Now, I just want a quick word about the profit-sharing scheme and then we can call it a day. What do you think of these new proposals that the Government's made? Should we consider them?'

Geoff drew in his upper lip and gazed thoughtfully at the papers before him. 'On the face of it, they do look quite good. There's a definite tax advantage. But having gone into everything, I'm not convinced. Our profit-sharing scheme is pretty wide ranging as it is. To incorporate these proposals would mean a separate scheme altogether and for the complexity involved I don't think it would be worth it. We're better to stay as we are.'

Felicity nodded. 'That was rather my impression when I looked them over. All right, Geoff, let me have the papers and I'll have a thorough look at them over the weekend. Well,' she rose and stretched herself, 'I now declare the week closed and the weekend open. Coming to the flat for a drink? I think we've got time, haven't we?'

'Sure thing.' Geoffrey came to his feet, looking appreciatively at Felicity's slender curving shape silhouetted against the window. 'I'll need to go back to change before we go out this evening, but there's a while yet. We got through pretty quickly this week.'

Felicity lowered her arms and nodded. She enjoyed these weekly sessions with her chief accountant, possibly even more than she enjoyed the evening out that so often followed. They had fallen into the habit of taking Friday night off together whenever possible, sometimes visiting Torquay or Exeter for a show or a concert, sometimes just going to a quiet country hotel for a meal. It was one of the few relaxations that Felicity allowed herself before a weekend that was as likely as not to involve more work.

'By the way,' she said as she led the way to her private flat at the other end of the castle, 'that artist we spoke about came this morning. Odd sort of man.' She spoke casually, not mentioning that it had taken her most of the rest of the morning to fight down her unexpected reaction to Jake Ashton. In any case, she had finally suc-ceeded in persuading herself that it was the result of a poor night's sleep and nothing else, nothing to do with Jake Ashton at all.

'Well, you'd expect an artist to be odd, wouldn't you?' Geoffrey waited while she unlocked her door. 'I suppose he turned up with long flowing hair and smothered in chains. D'you think he'll make a good job of the picture?'

'Yes, as a matter of fact, I think he will.' The living room waited for them, furnished in the practical, almost minimalist style that Felicity felt best befitted a woman who was managing director and chairman of a rapidly expanding company. Not wishing to lose the confidence of the clients and colleagues she occasionally brought here, she had successfully hidden her own preference for a more feminine style – so successfully that she barely remembered its existence herself, now. She waved Geoffrey to a deep, leather armchair and moved across to the drinks table. 'The usual?'

'Please.' He waited while she poured. 'So – what was he like?'

'The painter? Well, not odd in the way you suggested, though I must admit, that's what I expected too: the Bohemian image.' Felicity sipped her own drink. 'No, he looked quite normal – casually dressed, but I suppose he didn't see the need for a suit and tie to convince me he could paint. But there was something about him...' She frowned. 'I can't quite put my finger on it. I suppose it was his attitude more than anything. He seemed to think differently from the people I usually meet. This place, for example' – her waving hand encompassed the entire castle and its grounds – 'he seemed to be implying that it was better off before we came.'

'The man's a fool,' Geoffrey stated positively. 'And an insolent one at that. We'd better find someone else for the job.'

'No. I don't want to do that.' To her surprise, Felicity found that she most definitely did not want to do that. 'It doesn't really matter what he thinks, after all, does it? So long as he paints a good picture of the Board.'

'But can we be sure he'll do that? Once he's got the commission... Of course, we'll make the final payment dependent on whether we like what he produces, that goes without saying,' Geoffrey said shrewdly, but again Felicity shook her head.

'I don't think we can work that way, Geoff. We ask him to paint a picture on the understanding that he paints it his way. This isn't like decorating a room. He's got to do it the way he sees it, feels it.' She stopped, surprised at herself, and found Geoffrey staring at her in astonishment.

'Don't tell me he's brainwashed you with a lot of fancy ideas about creativity!' he exclaimed. 'Look, if we end up with some abstract monstrosity, with only half a face each or something–'

Felicity burst out laughing. 'I don't think he's going to do that. In fact, having talked with him I suspect he's more likely to paint us all with two faces– No, that was a joke,' she added hurriedly, seeing Geoffrey's face begin to turn scarlet. 'I'm sure he's going to paint a perfectly normal picture, once we've decided on the setting.'

'Why, it'll be the boardroom, of course. That's the normal thing.'

'Mm, I know. But our boardroom's such a cold room, Geoff. I've felt it before and it seemed even worse today, looking at it with Jake Ashton. He suggested–'

'*Cold?*' Geoffrey broke in. 'What on earth does the temperature matter in a *painting?* You're not making sense, Felicity – what's this man done to you?'

Privately, Felicity would have liked an answer to that question herself. But Geoffrey's attitude was putting her on the defensive. She wished now that she had never called Jake Ashton 'odd'.

'He hasn't done anything to me,' she said

stiffly. 'As I was about to tell you, he suggested using my office as a setting, with all of us in there having an informal discussion. We did also discuss the Great Hall–'

'Now that's a much better idea. The Board of Directors having their annual dinner – yes, that could look very good indeed. Your office' – Geoffrey snapped his fingers – 'no, it would give quite the wrong impression.'

'Why? What's wrong with my office? It's a very fine setting.'

'Oh, as offices go, it's a superb one, I'll grant you that. But what kind of impression would an 'informal discussion' give? All those armchairs, only your desk to indicate it's a work situation at all. It would look like an after-dinner gathering in a London club. Except that women–'

'Still aren't allowed in many London clubs,' Felicity said smoothly. 'And certainly not sitting behind large, imposing desks. Well, as it happens, Geoff, I think Jake Ashton's idea is quite a good one. I'll put it to the board, of course, but if it comes to a casting vote I shall certainly support it. Another drink?'

Geoffrey shook his head. His mouth was set in a thin line. He passed a hand over his smooth blond hair and rose to his feet.

41

'No thanks. I'll have to be going now if I'm to be ready to come back and pick you up by seven. You know, it would be a lot easier if I brought my things to change into here when we're going out early. Especially with the holiday season beginning – you know how crowded the roads can get.'

'Mm, well, we'll think about it,' Felicity said vaguely. Geoffrey had made this suggestion before and so far she had successfully resisted it, even though she could see his point. But to have Geoffrey here, showering and changing while she too was trying to get ready to go out – no, it would involve an intimacy she wasn't ready for. Didn't know whether she'd ever be ready for. Besides, that short period of solitude when he had gone was all the time she would have to herself in the whole day. It was too valuable to give up. But as Geoffrey prepared rather sulkily to leave, an idea struck her – one that would dispose of a problem that was likely to arise later on in the evening too.

'Look, it's silly for you to come all the way back here to pick me up,' she said. 'Especially with the traffic getting worse. Why don't I come and pick *you* up?'

'Nonsense. I'll come back for you.'

42

'It does make more sense that way,' Felicity pointed out. 'Your house is on the way, after all. Or perhaps we could meet at the cinema – it's only half an hour's drive to Exeter.' She glanced at him under her lashes, knowing he would never agree to her second suggestion.

Geoffrey hesitated, then gave in. 'All right, you come for me. But I don't like it – it means you'll have to drive back here alone afterwards...' He hesitated again and Felicity spoke quickly, before he could have any other idea.

'Geoff, I drive back here at night alone several times a week. Don't be an old woman – and don't be so chauvinistic. There's nothing wrong at all in going in my car for once – it means you'll be able to have an extra drink, too.' She wondered belatedly whether that was quite such a good suggestion. Geoffrey could grow embarrassingly amorous when he had had an 'extra' drink. Well, at least she'd succeeded in preventing him from coming back here. On neutral ground she would have no problem in coping with him. 'I'll see you at seven,' she concluded, and gave him a bright smile. 'And we're eating after the film, right?'

'Yes. I've booked a table at that new restaurant they speak so well of.' Geoffrey moved towards the door. 'Should be a good evening.' He looked at her as if about to say more, but she forestalled him with another bright smile and a small movement of farewell. 'Well, see you later, then.'

Felicity watched him go, then sank into her own armchair, closing her eyes. She was beginning to regret the friendship that she had allowed to develop between herself and Geoffrey. It had been pleasant enough at first, a casual sharing of interests and spare time, but she sensed that for Geoffrey it was beginning now to mean something more. She had an uneasy feeling that he would soon be asking her to make decisions – even a choice. A choice she wasn't at all sure she was ready to make.

Later, however, freshly showered and wearing a silky dress that skimmed her body and whispered luxuriously around her slim legs, Felicity felt more relaxed and back in command. As she drove to the 'executive cottage' Geoffrey had bought in a nearby village, she wondered idly just why she had felt so unsettled today. It couldn't really have been that painter. After all, he was only going to be a part of her life – she frowned at the phrase – for a very short time, and then only on the fringe. Perhaps she needed a break. It might be a good idea to go and see her father again; spend a few days in the mild air of Bournemouth. There were several things she wanted to discuss with him, anyway.

Geoffrey met her at the door and drew her inside, his eyes moving over her with approval.

'I like you in that colour. It makes your eyes look as if you were by the sea. What d'you call it, green or blue?'

'Aqua,' Felicity said with a smile. 'And I'm not saying any more than that. D'you know that men and women perceive colours differently? If I were to say this was green, you'd probably think it was blue.'

'And so it would be,' he grinned. 'Now, are you going to have a drink before we set out?'

'Not if I'm driving.' Felicity followed him into the lounge. 'Hullo, is that a new music centre? What was wrong with the old one? You'd only had it a year, surely.'

'This one's got some features the old one didn't have.' He moved over to show it to her. 'The CD's streets ahead. Listen to this.' The room was filled with the sudden blare of music. 'I don't really know why we bother going to concerts when we can get this kind of playback.'

'Because there's nothing to compare with actually being there.' Felicity moved around the room. 'Geoffrey, I've never known a man with so many gadgets as you've got here. Do you really use them all?'

'Of course I do. Watch this.' He picked up a small remote control box from an assortment on a small coffee table and pressed a button. Immediately a steel and plastic object shaped like a diminutive waiter appeared from a corner, bearing a tray of glasses. It made for Felicity, who gave a little scream and skipped out of its way, stopping on the exact spot where she had been standing. It raised the tray on a somewhat jerky arm and stood still.

'Take a glass,' Geoffrey said, and Felicity, casting him a dubious glance, reached forward and tentatively removed one of the glasses. The waiter immediately set out again, moving a yard or so before making another stop and lifting the tray again.

'Marvellous at parties,' Geoffrey observed. 'Only thing is, you've got to remember to keep supplying fresh glasses or it offers everyone their empties back.'

'And meanwhile you're stuck at the bar filling up while your tame Dalek gets all the fun of circulating with the drinks,' Felicity remarked dryly. 'Geoff, you're not serious! You don't really use this thing, do you?'

'No, not really,' he confessed. 'Someone lent it to me for a few days – hoping to get some business I suppose. I don't think I'll be ordering any.' He glanced at his watch. 'Well, we'd better be going.'

They went out to where Felicity's car stood on his tiny gravel drive, and Geoffrey paused by the driver's door. 'Er ... ?'

Felicity gave him a sweet smile. 'It's all right, thanks, Geoff. I don't mind driving tonight.' She allowed him to open the door for her and slid behind the wheel, while Geoffrey went round to the passenger's side. 'Now, tell me what this film is that we're going to see. All I know is that it's Dustin Hoffman's latest, so it's sure to be good.'

The film did indeed turn out to be very enjoyable, and they came out of the cinema discussing it with some animation. As they emerged into the night air, Felicity drew a deep breath of appreciation.

'What a lovely evening! It's so warm. Can we walk to the restaurant, Geoff? It's not far from here, is it?'

'Only a few minutes.' He took her arm to guide her through the crowd of people spilling out on to the pavement. 'Hope you're good and hungry. I could eat the proverbial horse myself, though I don't think we're going to be reduced to that at this place – it's collecting quite a gourmet reputation.'

'I can understand why,' she agreed a few moments later when they were settled at their table and she was studying the menu. 'How does anyone ever choose? I'm going to be here all night just wondering what to have!'

'Well, I'm not,' Geoffrey said. 'The soup for me, followed by a steak, as rare as they can make it. That shouldn't take long!'

'And sounds very much like the horse you were prepared to eat. I think I'll have fish. The turbot, please,' she said to the waiter. 'And the walnut and stilton salad to begin with.'

'Wine, madam?'

'Just one glass of white, medium dry. No, no more than that, Geoffrey, I've got to drive, remember? You'll need red anyway, to go with your steak.'

'A bottle of number 45 then,' he ordered,

and gave Felicity a half-defiant look. 'I might as well get some pleasure out of being a passenger.'

'Not very flattering to my driving,' she murmured with a twitch of her lips. 'In fact, I don't remember anyone having to get themselves drunk before they'd trust themselves to me! All right, Geoff, it was a joke. And now we've ordered, let's have a look around. The decor's very attractive, isn't it?'

The restaurant was like a moonlit wood, subdued lighting glimmering down between a ceiling of hanging plants. The sylvan effect was echoed by the tall weeping figs and potted birches that stood by the walls and between the tables, giving the kind of privacy that might be found in remote forest clearings. The flickering light of the candles on each table were like fireflies in the warm darkness of a tropical evening.

'I almost expect to see a deer peering out at me through the leaves,' Felicity said softly. 'In fact, I'm sure I can – oh!'

'What's the matter?' Geoffrey asked as her eyes widened and she stared at something just past his shoulder. 'You haven't really seen a deer, have you?' He laughed.

'Not a deer, no, but...' Felicity watched as

49

the man at the next table, whom she had glimpsed only briefly, came round the hedge of greenery and approached their table. 'Well, imagine seeing you again, Mr Ashton! You're the last person I'd have expected to meet here.'

'Am I really? I wonder why?' He stood tall and lean above her, looking down with grave brown eyes, and once again Felicity experienced that odd sensation, as if she were falling from somewhere very high into unimaginable depths. 'Do you think it's too sophisticated for a poor artist?'

Felicity blushed and was glad of the subdued lighting. 'No, of course not! It's just – well, it seems strange to meet someone twice in one day, when you've only just met them for the first time.' She caught herself up, biting her lip with annoyance at her incoherence. 'Stupid, of course. We might have been in the same place hundreds of times without knowing it.'

'Oh, I think I'd have known it.' He let a moment or two pass while his words sank into Felicity's brain, then he added casually, 'You're not easy to forget, Miss Grant. Especially to a painter's eye.'

Felicity stared up at him. Once again, he looked different from anyone else, his striking darkness set off by the dark burgundy velvet jacket he wore over a glimpse of peacock-blue waistcoat. Taller than most of the men present, his bearing might have been mistaken for arrogance. But Jake Ashton, she suspected, wasn't sufficiently interested in other people's opinions of him or his way of life to bother about being arrogant.

She swallowed. No other man she had ever known had had this power to reduce her to speechlessness, and she didn't like it. She sought for words and waved a hand across at Geoffrey.

'Geoff, this is Jake Ashton, the painter – you remember I mentioned him?' That ought to help put him in his place. 'Geoffrey Hall – a senior member of my Board.'

Jake Ashton turned at once, his eyes sharp with interest. 'Really? Then I'll be painting you too.'

'I'm afraid so,' Geoffrey said with mock sympathy. 'Not nearly such an attractive proposition as painting Miss Grant, I fear.'

'Oh, that's not so at all. That is the interesting thing about this commission – the chance to paint so many different characters. I'm not a chocolate-box artist, you know – a portrait needs more than a pretty face to make it memorable.'

And that's put me in my place, Felicity thought wryly. 'Mr Ashton wants to see us in action,' she said to Geoffrey. 'So he's going to sit in on the next two Board meetings. And he'll want to spend some time with each member individually.'

Geoffrey frowned. 'Is that necessary? Can't we just pose for you, in whatever setting is finally decided on? And while we're on that subject, I must say I don't agree with your idea of having it in Feli– Miss Grant's office. Seems quite the wrong setting to me. The boardroom is by far the most appropriate or, failing that, the Great Hall. I can't quite see–'

'Geoffrey, not now.' Felicity reached across the table and touched his hand. 'Mr Ashton didn't come here for a business discussion, and neither did we.' She gave Jake Ashton an apologetic smile. 'We came to see the new Dustin Hoffman film. Is that what you came for too?'

The artist shook his head. His eyes were on Felicity's hand still covering Geoffrey's, and she hastily removed it. 'No. I came for the opening of a gallery in the cathedral precinct. Friend of mine's trying a new venture. It attracted quite a good crowd, I'm pleased to say, so now we're celebrating.'

'Oh yes, I read about that. Well, I hope it does well. Will you be exhibiting any pictures yourself?'

'I doubt it. I don't go in much for that kind of thing.' He glanced over to the plants concealing his table and lifted his hand to the face now peering through the leaves. 'And I'd better go back. My friend's beginning to wonder where I've got to. Nice to have met you, Mr Hall. Miss Grant – I'll wait to hear. Have a pleasant evening.'

'Thank you,' Felicity said, trying to keep her voice cool. 'I'll be in touch, Mr Ashton.'

'Jake,' he said, half-turning before he disappeared once more into the greenery. 'Everyone just calls me Jake.'

'Jake,' she said faintly, but he was gone.

'Well,' Geoffrey said after a moment. 'What d'you make of that? I see what you mean – he *is* an odd character.'

'How d'you mean?' Felicity had already wished she'd never made that remark, but she was curious to see what Geoffrey's reasons were for thinking the artist odd. 'He didn't say anything out of place.'

'Nothing out of place? Calling you a chocolate box?' Geoffrey snorted. 'The man has no manners at all. And then arguing about where the painting's to be set. Well, anyone ought to have known that this is neither the time nor the place for that kind of discussion. No, if you ask me, he's pretty hard put to it to find work and he's desperate for this commission – that's why he approached you. And that being the case, I'd have grave doubts about whether he's up to it.' Geoffrey leaned forward a little, fixing her with his light blue eyes. 'We don't want some amateur daub for this picture, Felicity. We want something good.'

'And I'm sure that's what we'll get.' Felicity thought back, trying to remember exactly who had said what. 'And he didn't bring up the subject anyway, Geoff – you did. He simply came over to say good evening.'

Geoffrey stared at her. 'You're very vociferous on this guy's behalf, aren't you? Not falling for the romantic gypsy element, I hope?'

Felicity felt her face grow warm. 'Of course I'm not! I have nothing in common with him, nothing at all. I don't even understand art. I'm just trying to be fair.' To her relief, she saw their waiter approaching with a tray. 'Anyway, here's our first course – let's forget Jake Ashton and enjoy the food. Good heavens, what an enormous salad! And your soup smells delicious.'

Mollified, Geoffrey waited while the waiter placed their food in front of them. He tore off a piece of bread and picked up his spoon, then gave Felicity another searching glance.

'All the same,' he said, 'I'm not at all sure it's a good idea to have Ashton sitting in on Board meetings. There's a lot of confidential stuff discussed there, you know. How can we be sure he won't go giving secrets away to one of our rivals? For all you know, that may be why he's after the job. Oh, I daresay he's some sort of artist, but what credentials does he really have? We don't want to expose ourselves to industrial espionage.'

'Geoffrey, don't be ridiculous!' Felicity exclaimed. 'Andrew recommended him – do you think he'd be sending in spies? And I've talked with Jake quite a lot today and I'm quite certain he's straight. He convinced me, anyway.'

'That's the whole point of confidence tricksters and spies,' Geoffrey muttered. 'They convince people. I think I ought to have a word with him.'

'No!' The force of her denial shocked Felicity herself and she was conscious of a sudden silence from the tables nearest them. Lowering her voice, she went on fiercely, 'Look, I haven't come this far without developing a fairly good sense of judgement of people, and I'd swear Jake Ashton is as straight as they come. And a good painter. That doesn't mean I have to like him,' she went on quickly before Geoffrey could make any further sneer, 'but personalities don't come into this. He says he can make a good job of this painting and I believe him. As for hearing our secrets – well, we can always ask him to leave if there's anything particularly confidential being discussed, and in any case I doubt if he'll hear much of what goes on – he'll be too busy sketching.'

'You may be right,' Geoffrey said dubiously. 'But I hope he's not going to be around too much. He's unsettled you already. God knows what a week of having him hanging round the place is going to do. Especially if he decides he's got to spend most of it in your office.'

A similar thought had occurred to Felicity. It brought a strange, cold little shiver to her spine and a tremor somewhere deep inside. It also brought her to a decision.

If she were to have a break from work –

and she certainly needed one – there couldn't be a better time than after the next Board meeting was over, when Jake Ashton would have met them all and mapped out his timetable. She could do without his watchful presence in her office, so if he had to be there, she would be far better off somewhere else. She would go to Bournemouth then, and spend a few days with her father.

Occasionally, during the rest of the meal, she glanced past Geoffrey's shoulder, letting her eyes stray casually to that clump of greenery behind which Jake Ashton sat with his friend, the owner of the new gallery.

She caught no more than a glimpse of either. But as they rose to go they passed through the shadows close to the table where Felicity and Geoffrey were enjoying their last course. But it was enough to confirm what she had thought from that first glimpse, when the leaves had been parted to allow a pair of wide blue eyes to peep through in search of the errant artist. Jake Ashton's friend, the gallery owner, was tall, blonde and female.

And quite stunningly beautiful.

'Going to see your father? Good idea.

57

Though it's likely to prove something of a busman's holiday. I know you two when you get together, you talk of nothing but work!' Geoffrey gave her an affectionate grin and reached out to rumple her smooth hair. 'What do you say, shall we drive down and have dinner on the way? I know a very good place in the New Forest.'

Felicity looked at him and shook her head. The rest of the Board had left after the meeting and she was tidying her desk ready for the afternoon's work. Jake Ashton's appointment had been confirmed and the use of Felicity's office as a setting agreed, not without some heated discussion. Jake himself had been present for part of the meeting, still somewhat against Geoffrey's wishes, and had spent the time observing each member in turn and making quick sketches. He had now retired to the small room which had been assigned to him as a studio.

'I'm sorry, Geoff,' she said quietly. 'I'm not inviting you this time. I want to have a bit of time to myself, as well as with Dad. I need a complete break with the office – and all that's associated with it.'

He stared at her and she could see that he was affronted.

'Well, if that's the way you want it...' His voice was chilly. 'Naturally, I don't want to butt in.'

Felicity sighed. 'It's not that, Geoff. You wouldn't be butting in. It's simply that – well, with you there we won't be able to talk about anything but work, and I don't want that. I really don't. I need to recharge myself.'

'I do know how to relax as well,' he pointed out. 'I thought our Friday evenings together had proved that.'

'Yes, they do, but–' Felicity stopped helplessly. 'Look, let's leave it, shall we, Geoff? It's only a few days. I'll be back on Wednesday.'

'As you wish.' He was still offended, she thought sadly as she watched him go through the door, his shoulders rigid. And she really hadn't meant to hurt him. But it was impossible to tell him the truth. That she was afraid that if he came with her to visit her father, both men might read far more into the situation than she wanted. Geoffrey, in particular, might look on it as an opportunity to ask her to make that decision, that choice, which until now she had successfully avoided.

It was even more impossible to tell him

that, until a fortnight ago, she had been gradually coming round to his way of thinking, that she might even have been willing to make the decision he wanted. So what had happened to make her draw back now? In that time, nothing, except that Jake Ashton had come into her life. And it couldn't be anything to do with him.

Felicity had intended to drive directly from work to her father's house, but somehow by the time she had cleared her desk, gone to her flat, done a few chores, watered the plants and packed, it was well into the evening and she knew she would need at least a snack. She opened the fridge door and hesitated. Even boiling an egg seemed to be too much effort, and there was no milk or bread. I'll get something in the village pub, she thought. It'll be more relaxing, and then I can go straight off.

The Stallymore Arms was a small, old-fashioned inn, built in the sixteenth century, with all the charm of thatch, inglenook fireplace and low, beamed ceilings that usually cried out to be subtly smartened up, furnished with polished horse brasses and turned into a fashionable watering-hole. But Bill, the landlord, had stubbornly resisted such new-fangled ideas and kept his pub as it had always been – plain, honest and a meeting place for villagers rather than braying tourists.

'Hello, Miss Grant,' he said as Felicity came in. 'You're my first customer tonight. Hot enough for you?'

Felicity smiled and leaned on the bar. 'Nearly. I think I must have been a lizard in a previous life. Half a pint of cider, please, Bill, and some of your wonderful crab sandwiches. I need sustenance for the drive to Bournemouth.'

'Going to see your dad, are you?'

Felicity took the glass he handed her and took a sip. 'A few days away from the rat race. Somehow, I always feel less stressed at Dad's – although it's odd that I find Bournemouth restful when it's really so much busier than here.'

'Stallymore's quiet enough, in all conscience,' Bill remarked. 'I wouldn't have thought you'd find a place like Bournemouth restful, with all that traffic and bustle.'

'Well, there isn't any of that at Dad's house. He lives up on the cliff, with a big garden all round, so you can forget about the town. And of course there's no office

61

there – you're not aware of work waiting to be done a few doors away.'

'Perhaps you create your own stress at Stallymore,' another voice remarked, and Felicity whirled round with a gasp of surprise. Jake Ashton's brown eyes met hers, apparently grave but with a wicked twinkle dancing deep within them. 'What a shame,' he continued with a glimmer of a smile. 'It seems almost a crime, doesn't it, to take a beautiful place like Stallymore Castle and turn it into a stress zone.'

Felicity recovered herself, wondering at the same time why his sudden presence should have had such an effect on her. Anyone could walk into a pub. She gave him a cool glance and said, 'I don't think that's a very accurate description. Stallymore always seems very calm and efficient to me. But there's inevitably a certain tension about a workplace.'

Heavens, she thought, how can I sound so pompous? But Jake only grinned and settled himself comfortably on a bar stool beside her, nodding to Bill who began to draw him a pint of beer. 'Well,' he said, 'you're probably right. I obviously need to drift round the place quite a bit, to soak up the atmosphere. Calm, efficient, but with a certain tension – it'll all need to be there in the picture.'

Felicity sensed the touch of mockery in his voice and wished she hadn't used those words. I hope he's not going to use this picture to send us up, she thought uncomfortably, and remembered his encounter with Geoffrey earlier on. She wouldn't be at all surprised if he was tempted to send up Geoffrey. But how could you do that, in a straightforward portrait? A cartoon, yes – but not a picture like Jake Ashton had been commissioned to produce.

'It's all right,' Jake said as if reading her thoughts. 'I'm not going to make a joke of Grant Holdings. You'll get the picture you want.'

Felicity felt her face colour. 'I never thought–' she said in denial, but he only laughed comfortably and touched her hand.

'Well, you ought to have done. If I were you, I wouldn't trust me an inch. Would you, Bill?' He took the pint mug the landlord had slid across the bar and lifted it to his lips.

'Not an inch,' Bill said cheerfully, turning to go into the kitchen. 'See that up there, Miss Grant? That's supposed to me, if you'd believe it! Well, you tell me, is anyone going to recognise me from that daub?'

Felicity followed his gesture and burst out laughing. Pinned to a beam at the back of the bar was a sheet of paper with what appeared to be a swiftly drawn caricature on it. The caricature was of an elephant but it was equally obviously of Bill: completely bald, hugely fat, his long nose stretched to look like a trunk, a wide, friendly smile stretched between his large ears. The elephant held a foaming pint in one solid fist and a plate of sandwiches in the other, and as Bill came back from the kitchen carrying Felicity's supper, the resemblance was complete.

'Don't tell me you recognise me,' Bill said, sounding hurt. He set the plate of sandwiches on the bar. 'I reckon it's a conspiracy. Anyway, you'll laugh on the other side of your face when you see what he comes up with to hang on the wall of your boardroom.'

Felicity glanced at Jake in mock alarm. 'You don't really mean to show us all as animals, do you?'

'Well, it would be different, wouldn't it. And it might give you an insight into your own Board. Let's see...' He pursed his lips and narrowed his eyes. 'We might have a nice bland hippopotamus; a leopard, perhaps in the process of changing his spots; a crocodile, all smiles and sharp teeth; a cuddly bear with sharp claws; a hyena; a few intelligent, faithful dogs; and, of course, a magnificent lioness!' He grinned at her again.

Felicity stared at him. Her heart beat rapidly. 'You don't paint a very flattering picture of my Board,' she said at last. 'Crocodiles, hyenas, monkeys... Is that really how you see us?'

'I haven't had time yet to make up my mind,' he said. 'But on the whole, I think in any group of big business people you're likely to find a few of those characters. But don't forget the faithful dogs, and, of course, the lioness. Now that's what's going to make this picture really different – and really worthwhile.'

Felicity stared at him a moment or two longer, then turned her head away, still conscious of her beating heart. Despite his disclaimer, she couldn't help wondering which Board member he saw as a crocodile, or a hyena. A picture of Nigel Earnshaw's face rose in her mind, thin and dark and watchful. Which might he be?

'I don't think I want to go on with this conversation,' she said abruptly, and glanced at his pint jar, now almost half empty. 'You obviously come in here quite a lot, Mr Ashton. Cartoons on the wall, the landlord pulling your pint without even being told what you want–'

'Oh, I've been in and out of the Stallymore for years,' he said lightly. 'And the name's Jake.'

'So why haven't I seen you before?' she asked, adding hastily, 'Not that I'm always in the pub, but I do pop in from time to time. I'd have thought we'd have known each other by sight at least.'

'Maybe you've always been too occupied,' he suggested. 'I don't suppose you come in on your own much, do you? Incidentally, why are you here tonight? Don't you usually spend Fridays with the boyfriend?'

'The *boyfriend?*' Felicity said icily, and then, before he could say any more, 'As it happens, and not that it's any of your business, I'm on my way to spend a few days with my father in Bournemouth. I just dropped in for a bite before I go.' As if to prove her point, she picked up one of the crab sandwiches and bit into it.

'A very wise decision,' Jake said approvingly. 'Bill and Sue might not go in for smart cuisine but they certainly know how to produce a tasty sandwich.'

'I hope they go on doing it too,' Felicity said. The crab was fresh and delicious, the bread brown and home-made, the lettuce from Bill's own garden. 'This is far better than all your fancy dishes smothered in outlandish sauces.'

'I agree. And smart puddings with names like chocolate torture and strawberry and courgette delight. Give me good old bread-and-butter or Mum's apple pie any day.'

Felicity laughed at his choice of names. 'I can't imagine combining strawberries and courgettes.'

'Take my word for it, someone will, and what's more they'll make it and put it on some pub's menu. And people will eat it and exclaim over it. "Too perfectly scrumptious, darling!" While you and I will sit comfortably in Bill's little pub eating the best crab sandwiches on earth.' He gave her a smile and lifted his glass again. 'Good lord, it's empty. How did that happen? Bill – same again, please.'

Felicity continued to eat her sandwiches, feeling oddly shaken. The small exchange of jokes had made her forget, for a moment, some of the unsettling feelings that Jake Ashton always seemed to arouse in her. Instead, she'd felt comfortable, at ease, and somehow younger for a few minutes. As if some of the cares that had lain across her shoulders had been lightened. I never feel like this with Geoff, she thought. But then he doesn't have the same sense of humour. He just wouldn't understand. And he likes the sort of place Jake's just been making fun of. He likes smart cuisine and exotic puddings with fancy names.

'I'd better be going,' she said, finishing the last crumb and draining her glass of cider. 'It'll take me nearly three hours to get to Dad's, and I don't want to arrive too late.'

'Take care on the road,' Jake said, not moving from his stool. 'And have a relaxing weekend. I'll see you when you get back.'

'Yes.' She hesitated, but there seemed to be nothing more to say. Jake was watching her with that bright-eyed glance that made her feel as though he were simmering with amusement. Probably seeing me as some kind of Disneyland cartoon animal, she thought crossly – Minnie Mouse, perhaps or skinny Olive Oyl.

It would be a good thing to be out of the office for a few days, she thought, waiting in her car to let some more customers enter the parking area. Jake Ashton could spend the time in her office, making sketches or doing whatever it was he wanted to do, and by the time she came back he'd be studying the other board members or working in his little studio. She would hardly need to encounter him at all.

'You're looking better this morning,' John Grant observed at breakfast. 'You looked exhausted when you arrived last night.'

'I was later than I intended,' Felicity said. She drew up her chair to the table on the terrace and took a quarter of melon from the array of fresh fruit. 'And it's been a strange week. But I'm fine now – a good night's sleep works wonders.'

Her father poured coffee into a large white cup. 'How d'you mean, a strange week?'

'Oh, nothing really. The business is going well. It's just that we've got this painter in.' She giggled suddenly. 'Not decorators – though I think a team of men with ladders and wallpaper and pots of paint might well be a touch less disruptive! It's the artist we've commissioned to do a portrait of the Board. I've had to take him round the castle, show him the boardroom and all

69

that. He's – he's rather an unusual character.'

'Well, he's an artist,' her father said. 'He's bound to be a bit different from the kind of man you normally meet.'

Felicity frowned at the implication that she moved only in business circles, but realised that he was probably right. I ought to widen my social circle a bit, she thought, and wondered when she could find the time.

'I suppose I don't know quite what to expect from him,' she said. 'He seems to take me by surprise all the time. His opinions – they're different from other people's.'

'Sounds interesting. Tell me more.'

'Well, about Stallymore, for instance. He doesn't seem to like what I've done there at all. The gardens are looking their absolute best just now, but he seems to dismiss them as – as sort of chocolate-box gardens. Too prettified, too tidy. I get the feeling he'd really like to see a few weeds flourishing and a bit of shaggy grass.'

'Well, some people do prefer wilder gardens. There's nothing very unusual in that.'

'No, I suppose not. It's not just that, though. He thinks I ought to open it to the public. Share it. Have people walking about all over the gardens – through the woods.' She stopped suddenly, and then went on quickly. 'And it's the way he wants to paint the picture. He doesn't want us in the boardroom, or in the Great Hall, both of which would look really imposing, he wants it in my office, with everyone gathered round my desk. I don't know what the others are going to say. Some of them won't even be properly visible. And he wants it to look as if we're *arguing*.'

John Grant threw back his head and roared with laughter. 'Well, I can quite see some of them objecting to that! After all, no one is going to believe that Board members ever argue, are they! Sweetness and light, that's the image you need to project.'

Felicity gave him a suspicious glance. 'It's not funny, Dad–'

'I'm sorry,' he said, trying to pull the grin from his mouth. 'But you must admit it sounds funny, put like that. Look, you mustn't let this man get to you, Fliss. He's an artist, he's bound to be a bit different from the men you usually meet. But that doesn't mean to say he doesn't know his own job. He's got a good reputation.'

'I know.' She sighed. 'Well, I suppose the

best thing is to get the whole business over as soon as possible. Then he can go back to wherever he comes from and I won't need to see him again.'

John Grant regarded his daughter thoughtfully. 'And how's Geoffrey?' he enquired, apparently changing the subject.

Felicity shrugged. 'OK. He sent you his regards. He was a bit put out because I didn't ask him to come with me.'

'And why didn't you?'

'I didn't want him. I wanted to get away from work, forget it for a few days. You know what he's like, he can't talk about anything else, and he – well, he sort of takes over when he's here. Sits drinking whisky with you late at night, even expects me to make myself scarce while you and he have a glass of port after dinner. I feel like a little girl being sent out of the room while the grown-ups talk.' She gave him a rueful smile. 'I just wanted to have my dad to myself for a while.'

John smiled. 'And it's a pleasure for me to have my daughter to myself,' he said quietly. 'Geoffrey's a good enough chap, but you're right, he does take over. And don't you think he's just a touch pompous at times?'

Felicity thought of Geoffrey's behaviour

recently, at the restaurant where she'd introduced him to Jake. She smiled a little unwillingly, feeling guilty at discussing Geoffrey like this.

'Well – just a touch, maybe,' she said, and met her father's eyes. They were both laughing when Peggy, her father's housekeeper, came out through the patio door bearing a covered dish which she held with a cloth in both hands.

'A cooked breakfast!' Felicity exclaimed. 'Peggy, I never–'

'No such word,' the housekeeper declared, setting the dish on the table. 'And it's nothing much – just some scrambled eggs and a bit of bacon and a few tomatoes and mushrooms. You were looking really tired last night, Felicity, and as though you hadn't eaten properly for weeks.'

'Don't be silly. I eat like a horse. And I had some lovely crab sandwiches in the village pub before I left.' She remembered in whose company she had eaten the sandwiches and felt a faint blush colour her cheeks. 'This looks wonderful, Peggy,' she went on hurriedly as the older woman lifted the cover. 'And I'm certainly not going to refuse, after you've gone to all the trouble of cooking it.'

All three sat together in peaceful companionship, eating their breakfast and looking out over the gently rippling blue sea. A few yachts and sailing dinghies were already out there, sails like butterflies' wings skimming over the waves. A small plane was approaching, making for the little airport. Down on the promenade some of the people who had come to Bournemouth to retire would be starting to take their morning walks.

'And how are you, Dad?' Felicity asked after a while. 'Are you taking care of yourself?'

John Grant snorted. 'Don't get the chance!' He indicated Peggy, placidly eating scrambled eggs. '*She's* always behind me, nagging on about scarves and gloves and eating my greens. I tell you, I might as well have employed a nanny and had done with it. She'll be telling me not to suck my thumb next.'

'I'm not sure I would, if it meant you didn't always have that terrible old pipe stuck in your mouth instead,' Peggy said mildly. 'At least thumbs don't give you cancer.'

Felicity looked at them in sudden alarm. 'You don't mean–'

'No, of course not!' John glared at his housekeeper. 'What d'you mean by it, frightening my daughter like that? There's not a thing wrong with me,' he assured her, 'it's just Peggy fussing like an old hen as usual. You know what she's like.'

'I know you're lucky to have her,' Felicity said frankly, and looked at them with affection. Sitting there together at the breakfast table, they looked as comfortable and companionable as an old married couple. They had been together for years now, Peggy arriving as the last of a succession of housekeepers who had been variously unsatisfactory, and it had been as if John Grant had breathed a deep sigh of relief as she walked into the house, and settled down in contentment. Peggy too seemed happy, quietly running his house and slowly becoming more of a companion than a housekeeper. More, Felicity thought, like a wife.

'You ought to marry Peggy,' she told her father later when they were alone. 'Otherwise you may lose her one day.'

John looked shocked. 'Lose her? How?'

'Well, she might meet someone else,' Felicity suggested wickedly. 'Or just get herself a better job.'

Her father snorted, but he looked thoughtful and Felicity wondered if he had indeed been considering asking Peggy to be his wife.

In the afternoon, he went off to play his regular round of golf. Felicity declined the offer to go with him and stayed on the terrace instead, stretching out on the swing seat with a book and a cool drink. She read a few pages and then felt her eyelids droop. When she woke, Peggy was standing beside her with a tea tray.

'It's half-past three. I thought you'd better wake up or you'll never sleep tonight.'

'Oh, I will. I feel I could sleep for a month.' Felicity sat up and took the cup gratefully. 'Are you having one too? Sit here beside me, in the shade.'

'Thank you.' Felicity swung her legs off the seat and Peggy settled beside her under the cool canopy. Felicity picked up a home-made biscuit and nibbled it thoughtfully.

After a few minutes, she glanced sideways at Peggy and asked, 'Is Dad really all right? He's not ill, is he?'

'No, of course not. Why do you think-?' Peggy broke off and looked annoyed with herself. 'You're not still worrying about that silly remark I made about the pipe? No, there's no sign at all of anything like that.'

'What, then?' Felicity persisted gently. 'There's something you're not happy about, isn't there. Tell me, Peggy.'

The housekeeper frowned. 'I'm sure it's nothing, Felicity. It's probably just my imagination. He just seems – well, a bit tired these days. Nothing that a bit of rest wouldn't put right, but you know your father, he never stops while someone wants something of him. And people don't realise... He's on this committee and that committee, always out at meetings, always on the phone – it's worse than when he was running the printing works. He just does too much. He doesn't know how to say no.'

'He spent the whole morning sorting out papers and discussing some meeting he's going to on Monday,' Felicity said.

'I know. I wish he'd give a few of them up. Nobody's indispensable, I tell him, but he seems to think he's got an obligation to all these committees. Not much of an obligation when you're in your grave, I say.' Peggy reached out and covered Felicity's hand with her own. 'Don't take any notice of me! It's just a figure of speech. But I wish *he'd* take some notice.'

'So do I,' Felicity said. 'I thought when he

retired he'd take things easier – enjoy himself.'

'That's just the trouble, he does enjoy it. That doesn't mean it's not getting too much for him.' Peggy drank her tea quickly and reached for Felicity's cup to pour some more. 'I just wish he wouldn't keep taking on new responsibilities. The ones he took on to begin with were quite enough.'

'Well,' Felicity said decidedly, 'he'll just have to plead for time off while I'm here. I came to enjoy his company and that's what I mean to do, but I'm not going to trail round after him to meetings to do it! He seems to think I need a rest, so I'll go along with that -and make sure he gets one too!'

Peggy laughed. 'It's good to have you here, Felicity. He's always better for seeing you.'

'It's good to have you here too, Peggy,' Felicity said. 'You've been the best thing that's happened to Dad for years and years. I just hope you won't up and leave him someday.'

'Oh no,' Peggy said quietly. 'I'll never do that.'

Felicity had intended to put away all thoughts of work during her break, but her father was always interested in the business and confiding some of her problems in him seemed a good way to hold his attention. The next day they went for a long walk along the cliffs and she told him all about the members of the Board. There had been one or two new ones since he had last been to Stallymore, and he listened as she described them to him.

'And how about Earnshaw? How's he settling down now?'

Felicity frowned a little. Nigel Earnshaw had been with them for a year and she still knew no more about him than when he'd started. Thin, dark and silent, he gave her an uneasy feeling whenever she looked up during a Board meeting and found his eyes fixed on her. Once, she had come in and found him alone, standing behind her chair at the head of the table, lost in thought.

'I don't know. Oh, he does his work well – brilliantly – but I'm never sure I know what he's thinking. And he moves about so quietly – you come across him round corners, quite unexpectedly. Quite honestly, Dad, I don't really like him.'

'He's like his father,' John said. 'Very unobtrusive, but you could always rely on him to do the job and do it well. Sounds as if Nigel's a chip off the old block. You'll have to try not to let personal feelings cloud your judgement, Fliss.'

'I know. But there always seems to be something almost reptilian about him. Those dark eyes, and that long, thin neck. You know, I sometimes think he's got his eye on my job. If only he'd be more open.'

'His father was just the same. Played his cards right up against his chest. But you could trust him with the Crown Jewels.'

Felicity felt unconvinced. 'Well, I hope you're right. He just gives me a creepy feeling, looming at me out of dark corners.'

John chuckled. 'Well, you would set yourself up in a castle! How about Geoffrey? Apart from having his nose put out of joint through not being here this weekend?'

'Oh, he's fine. Keeping the figures under tight control. At least I don't have to wonder what he's thinking – with Geoff, what you see is what you get.'

'Hm,' John Grant said, sounding as unconvinced as Felicity herself had just done. 'Well, I don't know – he strikes me as being rather too self-satisfied. Perfectly reliable as long as he's getting what he wants – but what happens if he doesn't? He could be a very funny customer then, mark my words.'

Felicity laughed. 'Well, Geoffrey's getting what he wants. A smart little executive cottage, filled with high-tech gadgets – just wait till I tell you about his latest, Dad – a flashy car, and an excellent position with a lot of future. I don't think there's a thing that Geoff wants that he hasn't a very good chance of getting.'

'Isn't there?' John rested his eyes thoughtfully on his daughter's face. 'Isn't there really?'

Three

Felicity returned from her short holiday refreshed, all her confidence restored. A few days spent in the restful atmosphere of her father's house always did her good. She came smiling into her office, eager to see what progress had been made in the Haverford contract – and stopped dead at the sight of Jake Ashton sitting in an arm-chair in the corner, for all the world as though he owned the place.

'Hi,' he said as Felicity stood dumbstruck in the doorway. His lazy smile grew a little wider. 'Well, come in. You won't disturb me.'

Felicity drew a deep breath and closed the door behind her. She moved a few steps further into the room, never taking her eyes from him.

'*I* won't disturb *you?*' she managed to say, at last. 'Mr Ashton—'

'Jake, please.'

'Mr Ashton,' Felicity repeated firmly, 'perhaps I could remind you that this is my office. There's no question of my disturbing you – except to ask you to leave it. Now.'

'Oh, look here,' he protested, not moving, 'we agreed I should spend some time in here. It's the setting for the picture; you can't expect me to paint it from memory.'

'I expected you to do whatever it is you need to do in here while I was away. You've had plenty of time to do that now, and I'm sure you could work quite effectively in the room we've given you as a studio.'

'But I haven't been in here at all. There was no point, while it was empty.' He gazed up at her, his mahogany eyes bright and guileless. 'You see, a room as such has no interest for me at all. It only comes to life when there are people in it. And this room needs you. I'm sorry, but I have to be in here while you are or I simply can't do the job.' He smiled disarmingly. 'I really won't be any trouble to you, you know. I'll be as quiet as a church mouse. Or are they poor? I'm never quite sure. Anyway, I don't suppose they make much noise; nobody shouts in church, do they.'

Felicity felt suddenly as if she had not breathed for several minutes. She moved round her desk and sat down, afraid that her legs would give way if she didn't. She looked at Jake Ashton and felt helplessness wash over her.

'Mr Ashton–'

'Please,' he said with a coaxing smile, 'Jake. It's so much more friendly. And if we're going to be sharing an office–'

'Oh, all right, *Jake.*' She hadn't the energy to argue over that point. 'But let's get this quite clear. We're not going to be sharing an office. I simply can't work with you here. It's impossible.'

'Why?'

She made a small, frustrated movement with her hand. 'Well, because it is, that's all. I'm accustomed to working alone, or in consultation, not with an observer watching my every move. I'd be aware of you all the time. It just wouldn't work.'

'Funny,' he mused. 'The workforce seem

to manage all right.'

'What do you mean? You haven't been into any of our factories.'

'But I have.' His smile was really rather charming when he wanted it to be. She steeled herself against it. 'That's why I haven't been here. While you were away, I took the opportunity of going up to your printing works at Exeter. They had a team of workstudy experts there, observing people at work, time and motion study, that sort of thing. Not everyone liked being watched at their job, of course, but there it was, they had to put up with it. And you know, it was quite surprising how soon they got used to–'

'All right,' Felicity broke in, 'I get your point. But I still don't see–'

'Look,' he said. 'It's not just the room – I agree, I could do a lot with that when you're not here. It's you. I need to see you in the room, in action. If I'm going to paint you, I need to know you. To understand what makes you tick. Otherwise – well, the picture's going to be flat, two-dimensional. Can you understand that?'

'But pictures *are* two-dimensional,' Felicity said.

Jake laughed. *'Touché!* But I think you know what I mean.'

Felicity looked down at her desk. If she were to be honest, she had to admit she did know what he meant. But she still didn't like the idea of Jake Ashton sitting in a corner of her office, watching her every move.

'How long do you think you'll need to spend here?' she asked at last.

Jake shrugged. 'Can't really tell. A couple of days, perhaps. Could be a little longer. But I won't bother you any more than I can help.' He smiled again, showing very white teeth. He was looking cool and relaxed, his waistcoat – a bright blue one this morning – had been discarded and was tossed over a chair. He had pulled one of the small coffee tables in front of him that was already spread with large sheets of paper scattered with pencils. Felicity could see lines sketched on the paper.

He looked more settled in than she did herself.

'All right,' she said finally. 'If that's the way you need to work, you'd better stay. But no longer than necessary, all right? And please don't interrupt me while I'm working.' She still didn't see how she was to manage, making phone calls, dictating to Jackie, holding discussions, with him sitting there bright-eyed and curious. But as he'd pointed out, she expected exactly that of her workforce. And if this picture were to be painted, the sooner it was completed the better.

'Don't worry,' Jake answered her. 'I've my own time to consider too, you know. What is it you business people say? Time's money? Well, it's even more valuable than that to me. As for not being interrupted, I wholly agree. Nothing more irritating than people who keep looking over one's shoulder and ask how it's coming along.' His smile flashed again. 'So we're in complete agreement, aren't we?'

'Yes,' Felicity said, with a sense of tables being turned, 'I suppose we are.'

She pulled some papers towards her at random and stared at them without really seeing them. Out of the corner of her eye, she was aware of Jake's figure in his armchair, leaning forward over his own papers. His pencil seemed to be moving rapidly and she wondered what he was drawing. Herself?

She was relieved when Jackie came in with the morning post and sat down in the chair opposite to go over what had been happening during Felicity's break.

'Not too much to report. The sales figures

for last month have been agreed – we were up ten per cent on last year in self-adhesive labels, that new sort have gone very well, but packaging didn't do quite so well. We're still waiting for the final figures from GBM but the provisional ones look good. Oh, and Sir Michael Butterford's secretary rang – he wants a meeting with you as soon as possible over the Haverford contract.'

'Does he?' Felicity looked up sharply. 'I thought that was all going through without a hitch. Has something come up?'

'She wouldn't say. It didn't sound desperately urgent, but she did ask me to confirm an appointment as soon as you came back.' Jackie picked up Felicity's desk diary. 'I pencilled in Friday morning, if that's all right.'

'Yes, that'll do. Then I can talk with Geoffrey about whatever it is in the afternoon.' Felicity was still frowning a little. 'I'd better give Sir Michael lunch too. Book a table for us at the White Lion, would you? I'd still like to have some idea what he wants to talk about.'

'Well, it's only the day after tomorrow.' Jackie gathered up the letters she had been given to answer. 'Shall I come in for dictation in about half an hour?'

'Yes, that should be long enough for me to go through these.' Felicity picked up a report and began to study it. 'Oh, and let's have some coffee before you start, please, Jackie. I daresay Mr Ashton would like some too.'

'Yes, please,' came the voice from the corner. 'And there's no need for the formality. Jackie and I are firm friends now, aren't we?' Felicity glanced up in time to catch a teasing grin on his face and a blush warming Jackie's cheeks as she went hastily out through the door.

'You seem to have wasted no time in getting to know your way around,' she observed a little coolly, and was irritated to see the artist's grin widen.

'None at all,' he said cheerfully. 'In fact, I think I know my way around pretty well. How about you?' He went on quickly, before Felicity could think of a retort, 'By the way, I couldn't help overhearing – is that Sir Michael Butterford from Plymouth you were speaking of? The Curtis and Butterford figurehead?'

'As it happens, yes. And he's rather more than a figurehead. He's a very important man in the building trade.'

'I know. Well, that should be interesting.'

'Not for you,' Felicity said sharply. 'That's one occasion when you *won't* be in the office, Mr – Jake. Whatever he's coming to discuss, it'll be confidential and he won't want a stranger present.'

'Oh, but I'm not a stranger. Sir Michael and I have met before.'

'Oh.' Felicity was disconcerted but quickly rallied. 'I suppose you've painted a portrait of him. Well, I'm afraid that's hardly likely to make any difference.'

'Well, perhaps, perhaps not.' Jake's pencil was still moving busily and Felicity found the way he glanced up at her every few moments distinctly unnerving, even though his gaze was quite dispassionate. As if she were some kind of specimen of still life! she thought crossly. 'By the way, what's GBM?'

'GBM?'

'Jackie mentioned it. I hate these sets of initials, don't you? And they're even making words of them now. Yuppies, Dinkies. Whoopees – we'll all be so classified by initials soon we'll even have them on our passports. How would you describe yourself?' Even as he talked, he didn't stop working. 'Let's see, how would VBP do? That's Very Busy Person. No, not very good, I agree. I'll try to think of something better.'

He paused and looked up at her, and the sun flecked his eyes with gold. 'But you were going to tell me what GBM meant.'

'Was I?' Felicity had been gazing at him like a rabbit fascinated by a stoat. She pulled herself together. 'GBM simply means Grant Builders' Merchandising. It's one of our divisions. Nothing exciting or glamorous, I'm afraid.'

'No, it's not, is it,' he agreed. 'Don't you sometimes wish it were, Felicity? Don't you sometimes wish you worked in some other field – oh, perfume and cosmetics, perhaps, or fashion? You seem a little incongruous here, discussing builders' merchants and self-adhesive labels. I mean, not exactly riveting stuff, is it? If you don't mind my saying so.'

'As it happens. I mind very much!' she snapped. 'I get quite enough of that kind of attitude from the men I have to deal with. I don't need to get it from you. And if you don't mind, I have work to do. I thought we agreed on no interruptions.'

'Sorry, Felicity,' he said, not sounding in the least abashed. 'I thought you'd declared a coffee break – Jackie'll be in with it any second. But it'll be a stern silence from now on, if that's the way you want it.'

'It is. And I don't remember asking you to use my first name.' she added out of a frantic desire to squash that apparently irrepressible ebullience.

'You didn't. But you used mine, so I thought– But if you'd rather I went back to Miss Grant, which does sound to me rather like a schoolteacher–'

'Oh, don't bother. It really doesn't matter at all.' Felicity flapped a hand at him and turned back to her papers. Where was Jackie with the coffee? And how – how was she going to be able to work, with this dreadful man in the office radiating good humour at her whenever she happened to glance up, and behaving as though the concerns of a busy company had no more importance than – than the deliberations of a local cricket team?

However, after that, to her surprise, Jake Ashton behaved impeccably. He didn't interrupt once while Jackie was taking dictation, never spoke while Felicity was on the telephone and only at the end of the morning, as she put away the papers she had been working on, did he give her a bright, ironic glance that made her wonder just what he'd really been thinking during those quiet, busy hours.

'No roaming in the woods?' he enquired. 'It'd do you good, you know, half an hour out there with an apple in your pocket, listening to the birds.'

'It sounds delightful,' she said crisply. 'But I don't have time. I like to catch the one o'clock news on TV, and I'm expecting a call at one forty-five. You don't need to hurry back, though.'

'Oh, but I do,' he said easily. 'I want to catch a bit more atmosphere; you talking to one of your directors, perhaps, something like that. So if you're coming back at one forty-five, so shall I. Unless your call's private, of course.'

Felicity was tempted for a moment to tell him that it was. But what would be the point? He'd only be coming back again tomorrow – and perhaps next week as well. He was, quite clearly, determined to spend a certain amount of time in her office, and nothing she could do or say would prevent him. Not if the picture were to be painted.

Did it have to be painted? she wondered as she made her way along the panelled corridors to her flat. Would the Board really care if she abandoned the whole project?

But she couldn't do that. Not without giving them the impression she tried so hard to avoid, that of a vacillating and irrational female.

No. The picture had to be painted. And Jake Ashton was going to paint it.

They had been back in the office for just under an hour when Jackie buzzed to say that Geoffrey was in the outer office.

'Oh, good. Ask him to come in, please.' Felicity cast a slightly nervous glance in Jake's direction already anticipating Geoffrey's reaction when he saw the artist ensconced in his corner. But Jake only grinned cheerfully and waved his pencil at her.

'Don't let him bully you – he works for you, remember?' he remarked and, before Felicity could make any retort the door had opened and Geoffrey was inside.

'Hullo, Felicity. How did your weekend go?' He went on before she could answer. 'Look, we'll have to have another talk about the Haverford contract. I've just heard that Sir Michael Butterford's taking an interest. Now, why d'you suppose–' He became aware of Jake's presence and stopped. 'Ashton, I didn't realise you were here. Sorry, but Miss Grant and I have some business to discuss.'

'Well, I didn't suppose you were here to practise the latest disco-dance,' Jake observed. 'But that's OK, you go ahead. You won't disturb me.'

Felicity curbed a giggle. She looked at Geoffrey's face and knew that he was experiencing exactly the same reaction as she had during a similar exchange with Jake. At the same time, she was annoyed on Geoffrey's behalf. Naturally, he couldn't be expected to come in and behave as if Jake weren't there. And the talk was confidential – there had to be limits.

Geoffrey found his voice.

'Maybe not, but you'll disturb us. I'm sorry, you'll have to go.'

'But this is just what I need,' Jake said, his pencil flying across the paper. 'You and Felicity having a discussion. Any chance of a disagreement between you? I must be here for that!'

Geoffrey stared at the other man as if he couldn't quite believe his ears. 'Any chance of – no there's damned well not! Fel – Miss Grant and I are in total agreement over what we're about to discuss.'

'How d'you know that, if you haven't discussed it yet?' Jake's voice was bland, holding only mild interest, but it seemed to enrage Geoffrey even further. Felicity watched as his face turned dark red.

'Because I know the way Miss Grant thinks, that's how! And she thinks the way I do. When we've gone into all the ramifications of this affair, she'll agree exactly with the conclusions I've already drawn. Not that it's any business of yours – I don't even know why I'm bothering to talk to you about it.'

'But it is my business,' Jake told him. 'As long as I'm painting this picture, with Felicity and you, and the other members of the Board, in it, then I've got to make it my business. Don't think I'm interested in it for its own sake,' he added. 'From what I've seen today I'd find nothing more boring. But getting you all down on canvas when whatever it is that lights you up gets to work on you, now that *is* interesting.'

'I give up,' Geoffrey said. He turned to Felicity. 'Will you tell him to go, or shall I throw him out?'

'Neither.' Felicity gave him a cool look. She hadn't relished that assumption of Geoffrey's that she would automatically agree with whatever conclusions he drew. Did he really see her in that light? A yes-woman to his leadership, a mere figurehead?

'This is my office, Geoff, and Jake and I have agreed that for the next few days he should stay here and observe whatever goes on. Apparently it will help him get our characters right. I'm sure you'll agree that that's important.'

Geoffrey turned his pale blue eyes on her. 'You don't seriously mean to tell me that you believe that – that twaddle?'

'Why not? He's the artist. I know nothing about how artists need to work. If Jake tells me that's his way, I believe him.'

'So you really mean to tell me you're going to let him sit in that corner, watching and listening to everything that goes on? I don't believe this! Felicity, you've lost your senses. He's got you hypnotised.'

'Don't talk nonsense,' Felicity said sharply. 'Just forget he's there and tell me what you came for. I've got work to do, even if you haven't.'

'Yes, I daresay you have,' Geoffrey said grimly. 'Well, a conference with me isn't on the agenda – not while Ashton's sitting in that corner with ears like jug-handles, taking everything in. I'll talk to you later about this, Felicity, and about Sir Michael. Meanwhile, you know where my office is – we can talk there if you want to. Provided you come without your tame poodle!'

He turned and slammed out of the office. Felicity sat quite still, staring at her desk. Her heart was beating rapidly. It was the first time she and Geoffrey had ever seriously disagreed.

'That was absolutely great!' Jake Ashton said exultantly from his corner. 'You and Geoff really got going there for a moment, didn't you. Pity it didn't go on a bit longer, but never mind. It was just the kind of thing I need.'

Felicity turned on him.

'Oh, was it? Well, let me tell you this – it's not the kind of thing I need. In fact, it's the very last kind of thing either I or Geoffrey Hall or Grant Holdings themselves need. Now look' – she was on her feet, glowering at him, her grey eyes smouldering like ashes about to burst into renewed fire – 'I agreed to let you stay here on condition that you didn't disrupt my work. Now, I'm going to leave this office for a while and when I come back I expect to find you ready to keep to that condition. If not, it's out you go. And I don't care if your picture does look as if it's been posed by dummies. In fact, it might be a very good idea if you did use dummies!'

She swung round, her pale green skirt

flaring out round her knees, and stalked to the door. As she stretched out a hand to touch the knob, she heard Jake speak, his voice oddly humble.

'All right. I'm sorry. I apologise. I promise to be good.'

Felicity turned and looked at him suspiciously. But his expression was totally innocent, his eyes as honest as a spaniel's, and she felt her heart waver in spite of herself.

'Well – all right,' she heard herself say dubiously. 'But I mean it, you know. And I'm still going out.'

'Yes, of course,' he agreed deferentially. 'D'you mind telling me where? I mean, someone might wonder–'

'I do have a secretary,' Felicity pointed out. 'But if you want to know, I'm going to have a short walk in the grounds. A few minutes' fresh air might do me good.'

'That's the best idea you've had today,' he said approvingly, and put down his pencil. 'Why, I think I might even come with you–'

'Oh, for goodness' sake!' Felicity cried, and jerked the door open so hard that Jackie, about to come in with some papers, almost fell against her. 'I'm trying to get away from you, can't you see?' She disentangled herself from her astonished secretary and almost ran through the outer office, barely noticing the man who stood just beside Jackie's desk. It was only as she hurried down the stairs that she realised who it had been.

Nigel Earnshaw. The man she liked least of all her Board members. The man she sometimes suspected of waiting for her to make a false move, so that he could step into her shoes as Chairman and Managing Director of Grant Holdings.

The man she least wanted to see her behaving like a woman.

'I'm sorry to come here unannounced,' Geoffrey said, his voice sounding more belligerent than apologetic. 'But it seems that your flat is the only place where we can talk without that Ashton character hanging about.' He glanced round suspiciously, as if expecting Jake to leap from a cupboard waving a streamer. 'I really do think it's a bit much, letting him take over your office the way he has.'

'He hasn't taken it over,' Felicity said wearily. She wished Geoffrey would say what he wanted to say and then go. She hadn't been at all pleased to answer her garden door and find him standing outside. After a day that had left her feeling inexplicably tired, all she'd wanted to do was kick off her shoes and relax. Now here was Geoffrey, looking too big and purposeful to be shifted, evidently determined to talk shop.

Absently, she thought how odd it was that she had never noticed before just how much like a large white bull Geoffrey looked.

'Well, it's impossible to talk properly with him hovering in a corner like a witch's familiar,' Geoffrey grumbled. 'How long's it going to go on, has he given you any idea?'

'I don't know. A day or two, perhaps a bit longer. He's an artist, Geoff. He doesn't work within the same parameters as we do. He can't give exact estimations of time.'

'Doesn't choose to, you mean. Let's face it, Felicity, all this talk about the artistic temperament and creativity is just so much guff. They're parasites, the lot of them. Why, he could probably turn out a perfectly adequate picture in half a day – but if he did, he wouldn't be able to charge so much, would he? So he has to wrap it up with all this drivel about needing to watch you work, getting our characters right, absorbing the ambience – I ask you! And you're falling for it.'

'I'm not aware of falling for anything,' Felicity said stiffly. 'Look, Geoff, was there something special you wanted to say? Because if not–'

'Have you got someone coming?' Again, he cast a suspicious glance around the room. 'Far be it from me to intrude on your private–'

'No, there's no one else coming. It's nothing like that. Just that I'm rather tired and all I want to do is get under a cool shower and then do nothing for the rest of the evening. So–'

'You mean you're not doing anything special? Well, why not let's have dinner? We missed last Friday, remember, with you going to Bournemouth.'

Felicity looked at him. She had detected a plaintive note in Geoffrey's voice when he spoke about her weekend break and knew that he was still slightly offended that she hadn't taken him with her. If she refused to go out with him now...

'Please, Geoff,' she said. 'I really am tired.'

'Well, we needn't be late back. Tell you what, let's try that little pub we noticed on the back road to Crediton. Someone mentioned it to me the other day, said it's a good place for a bar meal. You don't want to have to get yourself a meal tonight if you're tired, and I know what you'll do – just eat an apple and a piece of cheese and call that dinner.' He glanced at his watch and she could see him expanding with the sense of being in control again. 'Look, I'll slip home and get out of this suit into something more casual, and I'll be back for you in – what? An hour? That long enough? And then we'll have a nice, quiet evening together, how does that sound?'

'Wonderful,' Felicity said dully, and watched him bound from the room. Well, at least someone was happy. And she really didn't have the energy to argue any more. Previous experience had taught her that if Geoff didn't win in the end, she'd be left feeling more drained than ever. It was simpler to give in.

As she moved slowly into her bedroom and began to strip off her business clothes, ready for the shower, she wondered just how many potential arguments Geoffrey had won in this manner. And if that was why he assumed that she would, inevitably, think along the lines he laid down and agree with the conclusions he drew.

She had never given way to him over a

business matter – at least, she didn't think she had. But had he, as their friendship grew, taken it for granted that she would do so, if a difference of opinion ever arose?

As Felicity stepped under the shower, she had a brief, vivid picture of Jake Ashton's face, watching Geoffrey and herself, bright-eyed, amusement and irony playing about those well-shaped lips, a sardonic remark just waiting to be uttered.

'Oh, go away,' she muttered crossly. 'Don't you ever know when you're not wanted?'

Geoffrey's idea of a quiet evening in a pub turned out to be a disaster on every count. For a start, the journey there through the narrow, twisting lanes had been slowed down by the fact that the road had been newly tarred and covered with loose chippings. Geoffrey, who had recently taken delivery of a new car and was inordinately proud of its silver bodywork, was clearly in agony at the approach of any other vehicle, his imagination peppering the car with marks as if it had been fired on by a shotgun. His sigh of relief when the chippings came to an end was echoed by Felicity's – and followed almost at once by a loud groan as they rounded a bend and found themselves behind a huge, lumbering tractor.

'This is the end!' he exclaimed. 'Look at that Heath Robinson contraption! What on earth *is* it, for God's sake? I mean, who needs all those spikes and that curly thing on the end?'

'Evidently farmers do. This farmer, anyway.' Felicity looked with amused interest at the extraordinary implement being towed by the tractor. 'I can't imagine what it does – shall we stop and ask him?'

'No, for God's sake don't make him go any slower than he is already. How far d'you think he's going? You'd think he'd have finished work by this time, wouldn't you? Be at home having his tea or whatever farmers have.' Geoffrey changed into bottom gear, swearing under his breath.

'Perhaps he has finished work,' Felicity suggested impishly. 'He might be going out for the evening in it, like some people use company cars.' A glance at Geoffrey's face told her that this little dig had not been appreciated. 'He could even be going to the very pub we're heading for,' she went on blithely. 'Or perhaps there's a rally on somewhere. A competition for the most unbelievable farm implement. We'll probably meet some more in a minute, even bigger and spikier and curlier than this thing. D'you know, I wouldn't be surprised if–'

'For God's sake, Felicity!' Geoffrey burst out, his face scarlet. 'It isn't funny, you know. How do you think I can concentrate on getting past this thing, with you burbling away in my ear?'

'Not funny?' she said. 'Well, really, Geoffrey, it's not that serious, is it? We're only going out for a pub meal, not having an audience with the Queen. And he's got just as much right to use this road as we have – more, probably. Anyway, you shouldn't even be trying to pass – it's far too narrow.'

That, she knew at once, had been quite the wrong thing to say. At the very next slight widening of the road, Geoffrey put his foot down, changed gear again and tried to thrust past the unwieldy vehicle lumbering along in front of them. Too late, he saw the hedges closing in again and braked. But one of the spikes caught the front wing on Felicity's side and they both heard the harsh grating sound as it scraped its way through the silver paint.

'Oh, no,' Geoffrey groaned. 'That's the last straw. I knew we ought to have gone the main road way.' And he slumped back in his seat and refused to speak again until they had finally shaken off the tractor at the next fork and driven on to the pub.

But by then, the evening's pattern had been set. The pub had changed hands since they had last seen it and the new owner had installed computer-games machines and a juke box. Pop music of the loudest kind competed frantically with the sound of electronic wars being fought across several screens, and the air was filled with the scent of basket meals and chips.

'I don't believe it,' Geoffrey said, staring around him. 'I don't believe anyone could do this. Well, we're not stopping here. We'll go on to Exeter, have a decent meal at the Royal. Come on, Felicity.'

But Felicity shook her head.

'I'm sorry, Geoff. I'm not going an inch further. I'm especially not going to Exeter. If you remember, I didn't want to come out at all tonight, but now we're here I'm going to have something to eat and drink. If you don't want anything, you can stay in the car till I've finished, and then you can take me home. And don't order me about as if I were your – your dog, or your wife or something!'

She marched through the door and forced her way through the crowd of young men and girls to the bar. She didn't even glance back to see if Geoffrey were following her. In her present mood, she wasn't sure whether to laugh or cry, but she had an uneasy feeling that if she said anything more to Geoff, it would be cry. Or maybe scream.

How would Jake Ashton have reacted to this evening's irritations? she wondered suddenly. And had a strong feeling that he wouldn't have seen them as irritations at all. Just something to laugh at, something to turn a disastrous evening into fun.

Fun. She tasted the word as if it were new. It seemed a long, long time since she had had any fun.

Four

'You know, I think you're beginning to quite enjoy seeing me around the office,' Jake remarked as they shared a pot of coffee a few days later.

Felicity leaned back and looked at him with a mixture of exasperation and affection. Affection? she thought in disbelief. Was that really what she felt for this man, who had forced himself so persistently yet gently into her life? Oh, no – affection implied that she saw him rather as she might see a large, friendly dog which insisted on bounding up to her and putting its big, heavy paws on her shoulders. And Jake Ashton wasn't at all like that. Flippant though he might be, she still had that sense that something rather dangerous lurked beneath the coloured waistcoat he always wore. Something that belonged in the jungle ... something panther-like...

'Where do you get all those waistcoats?' she asked suddenly. 'I've never seen you in the same one twice.'

'Oxfam shops, mostly,' he said carelessly, getting up to wander over to the window. 'You'd be surprised at the clothes they get in there. But I don't suppose you've ever been into one, have you?'

'I've sent things there,' she said defensively and then, in sudden concern, 'Look, d'you need any of your money in advance? I mean, you've been working here for nearly three weeks now, on and off. You started before the Board meeting at the end of May, and it's obviously going to be a while before you finish, so–'

To her surprise and faint annoyance, Jake

108

burst out laughing. 'What's the matter, afraid I'm starving? I don't go into Oxfam shops because I need to, you know! I can afford to dress – oh, anywhere. Marks & Spencer, BHS, Harrods, you name them I'm not ashamed to give them my custom. But none of those places have the kind of things I like.' He glanced down at her stiff face and grinned. 'It's kind of you to be concerned,' he said gently. 'But I'm quite all right, not destitute. And I don't really need a lot to live on. I don't have an expensive image to maintain, you see, so the snazzy car and the hi-tech gadgets aren't necessary.'

'Not like business people,' Felicity said, without thawing. She felt his hand on her shoulder.

'I'm not criticising you,' he said quietly. 'We just live in different worlds.'

Felicity sat quite still. It was the first time Jake Ashton had touched her since that first morning when they had shaken hands and she'd felt her skin tingling faintly at the contact. Now, it was as if she had been touched by a flicker of lightning. The sensation licked like fire along her arms, down her spine, into her heart, and set it kicking like a rabbit in a snare. She felt her face grow hot and then cold, and had to swallow hard and touch her lips with her tongue before she dared speak.

'You must know a good deal about my world by now,' she managed to say at last, huskily.

'Your business world, yes.' He took his hand away and she felt momentarily bereft. 'I suppose I know as much about that as anyone. And I appreciate the way you've co-operated over that – don't think I don't realise how hard it's been for you, having me lurking in that corner like an ever-present, all-seeing eye. But the rest of your life – no, that's still closed to me. What happens when you leave this office and go to your flat – with that little walled garden that's so inaccessible to prying eyes – what you're like when you take off the Miss Grant of Grant Holdings skin and slip back into Felicity the woman – no, that I don't know. I can speculate, of course,' he added, 'but I can't know.'

Felicity turned to face him as he leaned back against the window sill, his long body outlined against the brightness.

'Are you saying you want to follow me home now, sit in the corner of my private life? Is that what this is leading up to, Jake?'

He gazed down at her thoughtfully.

'An interesting way of putting it. And maybe a week or two, or three ago, I'd have said yes. It would certainly be quite invaluable for my work. But "sit in the corner of your private life" – no. I don't think it would stop at that now, do you? I'd want more than that. Much, much more.'

He levered himself away from the window sill and came close to her, leaning down to where she sat in her big office chair. Felicity, mesmerised, saw a hand come each side of her, planting itself firmly on the desk so that she was enclosed. She felt his warmth through the thin cotton of her dress, felt her heart kick again, and looked up slowly to meet his forest-dark eyes.

'Well?' he said softly. 'Do you dare? You take risks every day of your life in this office – why not take a few outside it as well? Or do you prefer to keep your private life as orderly and under control as that garden out there?' He gave her a long look, then pushed himself away and moved back to the window. 'Though it isn't all orderly, is it? Beyond that garden is the dark, dark wood, and all manner of secrets hidden there. Tell me, have you really never gone into the trees?'

Felicity found her breath. She moved briskly, finding reassurance in picking up and shuffling a pile of papers. Her voice, when she at last managed use it, came as casually as she desired.

'The woods? Oh yes, years ago. When we all used to come and stay here, my cousins and I.' She laughed. 'We called the garden a jungle, and so it was then. And the woods – well, they were just a tangle of undergrowth. We didn't actually go into them all that much.' But she had gone once, one afternoon when she was quite alone, she remembered. That was the day when she'd answered a strange impulse that had been urging her to explore between the trees, an impulse she never confessed to the others. She'd found a maze of narrow paths inside, paths made by animals, she supposed, and she'd followed them warily, keeping eyes and ears open for the bears and wolves her older cousin Andrew had told her lived there. But there had been no bears, no wolves – only the lake, stumbled on unexpectedly, dark and secret under the bending trees. The lake and the boy...

'I haven't been there for years now,' she said offhandedly. 'I'm not really very keen on wild places.'

'No?' His dark eyes were on her face. 'Are you sure about that, Felicity? Have you ever given yourself a chance? Or have you spent so much time in city streets and airports that you've forgotten what a wilderness is? Perhaps you've never even been in one except for that wood out there, years ago.'

'No, I don't think I have,' Felicity said coolly. 'And I can't say I've ever lost much sleep over it. As for city streets – I don't see too many of them round here.'

'Ah, but you don't really live round here, do you?' he said. 'Oh, I know you have a flat here, you go to bed here and get up again and do your work, but you aren't really, a part of the community, are you? You never walk down the village street, stand in line at the post office and exchange gossip with the neighbours. You wouldn't think of spending an evening at the local country-dance club, or helping out at the community centre fund-raising coffee evening. No, if you want an evening off you go to Exeter, and your real life is in the business world, which operates primarily around city streets. However much you may protest that you live in the country, you don't really. You've just brought a bit of the city to Stallymore Castle and wrapped it round you like a cocoon.' He gestured out of the window. 'Hence the orderly gardens, with not a blade of grass out of place. Why, it might as well be painted on!'

'I don't know what you think gives you the right to harangue me like this!' Felicity began furiously, but he smiled that infuriating smile and held a hand in the air, palm towards her.

'No need to get so cross. I'm not criticising, just stating fact. Your way of life could never be mine, but that doesn't make it totally invalid. I just think it's a pity you've shut so much else out of your life, that's all. So much that's beautiful and true. But that's your business. As for having the right to harangue you – why not? You're just an ordinary human being, like me, like the rest of us, not some distant goddess to be worshipped and kowtowed to.'

Felicity stared at him. He was leaning back again, smiling, quite at ease and unperturbed by her annoyance. She made a gesture of helplessness. How could she ever understand this man? He was quite unpredictable, at one moment filling her head with inane chatter and cracking silly jokes, the next making a series of amazing statements, apparently in all sincerity, that made her life look shallow and unreal. Yes, and that was the worst of it – she could actually see what he meant. She could almost believe him. And if that were really the case... She felt as if the earth were shifting beneath her feet, as if the entire fabric of her life were splitting. A tremor of fear shot through her.

'Any more coffee in that pot?' Jake enquired, as if nothing more momentous than an inconsequential chat had passed between them.

'Coffee?' she repeated dazedly. 'Oh – yes, I think so.' She watched as he poured. He held the pot over her own cup and lifted his brows interrogatively. 'Yes, yes please.' It might help to clear her head, at least.

'Well, so what do you say?' Jake continued cheerfully. 'Will this evening do? Shall I call in sometime during the evening? You say whatever time suits you.'

Felicity blinked. 'I'm sorry? I don't quite follow–'

'For this at home session we were discussing.' His tone was at its blandest. 'Remember, we agreed a few minutes ago that I needed to see you away from the work situation, as you are when you're relaxed. Don't dress up or anything, just put on whatever you normally wear when you're on your own, and do whatever you'd normally do. What is that, by the way – watching TV, listening to music, reading? Or maybe you play yourself at Scrabble or cook sumptuous gourmet meals for one. For all I know, you might make rag rugs or do carpentry. Anyway, whatever it is, you just carry on as if I weren't there.'

'Jake,' Felicity said carefully, 'you won't be there. When I have an evening alone, I like to spend it alone. D'you understand?'

'Oh yes, of course. But I don't count any more, do I? You've got quite used to my being in the office – you just look on me as part of the furniture now. It won't be any different in your flat, I promise you.'

Wouldn't it? Felicity looked at him, remembering those electric moments when he had touched her shoulder, leaned over her.

'No,' she said positively. 'For one thing, I just don't see the need. You're going to paint me here, not in my flat, and in my business dress, not a tracksuit or dressing gown. This is a picture of a company Board, not an in-depth investigation.'

'But a picture should be deep, if it's to succeed at all,' Jake said mildly. 'And I've only seen one facet of your personality so far. Well, perhaps a couple more, when you didn't think they were showing.' He laughed at her indignant expression. Then he spoke seriously. 'Felicity, it really is important that I see you at home. You see, I suspect that it's only there that you let your guard drop, where you let yourself be a woman – and it's the woman in you that I want to paint.'

'The businesswoman,' she said stubbornly, but he shook his head.

'The real woman. Otherwise this painting is going to be static, meaningless.'

She eyed him doubtfully. He'd used the same phrase before, when persuading her to allow him to sit in the office. Was it part of some ploy? Yet it sounded genuine enough – if you once accepted the principle of the creative mind.

Geoffrey hadn't accepted it. He had grown more suspicious as the days passed, and refused to hold any business discussions with Felicity while Jake was in the office. Remembering that, she wondered what Geoffrey's reaction would be if he discovered that she'd invited Jake into her flat for an evening. And hard on the heels of that thought came another.

Geoffrey didn't own her. But he'd been

acting more and more, just lately, as if he did. And if there was one thing that Felicity loathed above all else, it was possessiveness.

Why, after all, shouldn't she invite Jake Ashton to her flat if she wanted to? Particularly if it were for the sake of the picture.

'All right,' she said before she could change her mind. 'You can come along this evening. About eight. No – you might as well make it earlier. Come at seven and have some supper.'

'That's very generous of you,' Jake said, eyeing her in his turn. Perhaps he was surprised at her sudden capitulation. Probably put it all down to his fatal charm, she thought wryly. Well, he needn't think his charm would get him any further than that. Supper and a chance to see her at home, and that was it. And once only.

'Will you be doing this with all the Board members?' she asked as she swung her chair back to her desk and prepared to start work again. 'Following them home, I mean, as well as observing them at work?'

'Oh, no, that won't be necessary,' he said easily. 'After all, they'll mostly be little more than background figures. You're the important one, the leader of the pack. And your being a woman adds a tremendous – shall we say, intrigue? – to the whole set-up. That's why I'm taking so much trouble over you.'

Of course, Felicity thought, bending her head. It had to be for the picture's sake. In his way, Jake Ashton was as single-minded as she herself.

So why the slight feeling of disappoint-ment?

'So this is where you live.' Jake stepped inside the door and looked around the big living room. Felicity, watching his face with an anxiety she didn't understand, saw his eager expression die, to be replaced by something very like dismay. 'Oh.'

'Oh what?' she demanded tautly. 'What's wrong with it? I took a lot of trouble furnishing this room.'

'So I can see,' he said, and remained silent.

'I suppose you think it's like the garden,' she burst out after a moment. 'You think it would have been better if I'd left it as it was. Well, if you could have seen it when I bought–'

'Oh, I can believe it was a ruin then. Worse than Miss Havisham's bridal suite with cobwebs like curtains, and mice nesting in the cushions. You don't have to tell me. I suppose I was expecting something else. Something that looked – well, as if it had been allowed to grow around you. This looks more like an extension of your office.'

Felicity looked around at the leather armchairs, the stark, functional table, the prints on the white walls. It did look a bit soulless. But why should he have expected anything else?

'Well, now you know,' she said coolly. 'There aren't any more facets after all. You've seen them all in the office, and they're the same ones that I keep at home. There just isn't any more, Jake, all right?'

'No,' he said slowly, staring down at her. 'It's not all right. I don't believe it. There's more to you than this. There's someone inside you, Felicity, someone clamouring to get out. And if you don't let her out – and soon – you're going to be in trouble.'

Felicity met his eyes and felt an uncomfortable prickling of her skin. She turned away quickly and spoke with a flippancy she didn't feel.

'Oh, spare me the psychological bit. Now, if you want to make any sketches, you're welcome to do so while I get the supper. I've put a table there, ready for you, or maybe you think it's not worth stopping, now that you've discovered the real me.'

'Oh, I'll stay,' he said, and when she turned back she found that his eyes were still on her, dark and thoughtful. 'I don't believe I've discovered anything yet.'

Felicity shrugged impatiently and went into the kitchen, hoping he wouldn't follow her. Not that it mattered if he did – he wouldn't discover anything – but she desperately needed a few minutes alone to recover her composure. She was uncomfortably afraid that Jake Ashton had seen further through her disguise than any man she had yet encountered, and she didn't want to take any chances on his getting any deeper. If she could only get through this evening, she'd never let him in here again. He saw too much, surmised too accurately.

When she came out into the living room again, Jake was standing at the french windows, gazing out into the tiny, walled garden.

'Now this,' he said without turning, 'is something else. We're beginning to get a little closer here, don't you think?' He nodded his head at the riot of colour outside, the old-fashioned cottage garden filled with thrusting, jostling flowers that

121

Felicity tended herself.

'Closer to what?' She cursed herself for having forgotten the garden, then wondered just why she should be so afraid of Jake Ashton anyway. He was only an artist, after all, engaged to do a job of work. When the job was over (soon now, she hoped) he would disappear and she never need think of him again. Except when she looked at the picture, of course, and remembered.

'Closer to the muddy footprints,' he said, and turned to smile at her. Her heart paused. There was no irony in his smile now, no impishness dancing in his eyes. Instead, there was warmth, and an un-expected gravity, deep down, that seemed to speak to her in a language she didn't know but could almost grasp. Almost understand. 'Remember?' he said softly, reaching out a long arm to draw her close beside him at the window. 'The kids, the dogs, the muddy footprints? The noise and the laughter?'

Felicity stayed quite still. His arm en-circled her lightly, a flame burning across her shoulders. Once again, her memory took her back into the past, into long summer holidays spent here with her cousins. Into summer evenings when the sun went to bed late and the children were allowed to roam until they were exhausted. Afternoons in the tangled grass, by the green-smelling ponds, and wandering alone under the trees to a hidden lake...

'The garlic bread!' she exclaimed, wrenching herself away from him. 'I left it in the oven – it'll be burning.' And the memories dissolved and vanished as if they had never been conjured up out of a few words, a few ordinary phrases.

The meal was almost a success. Felicity served soup, followed by salmon steaks with small potatoes and broad beans from the kitchen garden, finishing with cheese and fresh fruit. Jake proved an impeccably mannered guest and soon had her laughing helplessly over his stories of some of the people he had been commissioned to paint. 'No names, no pack-drill,' he said with a grin, 'but really, it would be a crime to keep it all to myself. Don't you agree?'

'Oh, absolutely,' she said, still laughing. 'But I must admit I'm rather worried about what you'll tell your next sitter about me – I mean, us.'

'Grant Holdings, you mean. Oh, there's nothing to worry about there – I shan't give away any of your state secrets. No, if I talk about you at all it'll be about that incredible deal I heard you pulling off yesterday. I still can't believe I heard right, but you seemed to be swapping building equipment for tins of corned beef. Is that really what you were doing, or was it some code? Sounded crazy to me.'

'No, it's quite right,' Felicity said with a smile. 'You see, some countries don't allow their currency out, but they will allow what's called 'counter-trade'. So I sell building machinery and they pay me in corned beef, which I sell on to some grocery chain. Of course, if you do much of this it makes sense to own your own grocery chain, which is what we're looking into now – you might have heard us talking about the Haverford contract. Well–'

'Spare me, please,' Jake begged, holding up both hands. 'You lost me about five sentences ago. So they call it counter-trade, do they? When I was at school we used to call it plain, ordinary swapping. My king conker for your old football. Do all companies do this kind of thing?'

'Well, it depends what they're trading in, of course, but yes, quite a lot do.' Felicity got up and went out into the kitchen to collect the coffee. 'Finland bought some jet training planes from us – Britain, I mean –

and paid in vodka and liquorice all-sorts–'

'I don't believe it!'

'–and Russia paid for a computer in Christmas cards. It's not really all that uncommon.'

'And I thought big business was boring,' he said, shaking his head. 'We'll be back to shells and glass beads before we know where we are. Yes, please, I'll have some coffee– Oh God! Are you all right?'

Felicity, in the act of pouring the first cup, felt her wrist give way under the weight and gave a scream as the scalding liquid poured from the pot over her dress. She leapt to her feet, holding the material away from her legs, and felt Jake's arms round her before she was even aware that he had moved. Half-sobbing with shock and pain, she turned her face against his chest.

'Quick!' he said tersely. 'You'd better get that dress off. You're going to be badly scalded otherwise. Did it soak through?' He was pulling buttons undone as he spoke and lifting the dress over her head before she had time to protest. 'How on earth did it happen? No, never mind answering that. It's caught you on the thighs – look, the best thing for burns is cold water, straightaway. I'm going to put you under the shower.

Where is it?'

Felicity nodded her head at the bedroom door and he lifted her easily in his arms, thrusting the door open with one foot.

So he was in here after all, she thought briefly as he strode through the pretty, gold and white room with its flowery curtains and matching duvet, its scatter of lace-covered cushions. The only room in the flat which was truly hers, where she felt really at home -the room that expressed most the personality she concealed from everyone else, and the room she'd least wanted Jake Ashton to see.

But there was no time to think of that now. And Jake himself didn't seem interested. He jerked his head enquiringly.

'This door?' He set her down just inside the bathroom and pulled open the shower door. 'Don't bother about undressing – the important thing is to get some cold water on that scalded skin. In you go!'

Before she could say a word, he had thrust her into the shower compartment and turned on the cold water. Felicity gasped as the icy spray hit her body, then felt the relief as it touched her burning thighs. Within seconds, she was soaked, her hair streaming, her silk slip clinging to her body. Still half-crying, shaken by the swiftness of events, she stood shivering in the cascade, her eyes closed against the ferocity of the spray.

'How – how l-long do I have to s-stay here?' she asked through chattering teeth, opening her eyes momentarily to look at Jake, who was still standing at the partly open shower door.

'Until you're sure the burning's stopped, and then some. With any luck, you'll have nothing to show for it – it's surprising how effective cold water can be if it's applied quickly enough. And I shouldn't think more than about thirty seconds went by between you dropping the pot and my getting you in here. How did it happen?' he asked again. 'I didn't jog your arm, did I?'

'No, nothing like that. My wrist just gave way. It does sometimes. I sprained it once playing t-tennis and it never seemed to get quite as strong again. I didn't think about how heavy the p-pot was when I lifted it.'

'Well, you'd better make coffee in smaller quantities next time,' he remarked. 'How's it going? Don't freeze to death in there, will you? I don't want to have to call the doctor out to treat you for hypothermia.'

'Not after having s-saved me from b-burning, no,' she agreed. She opened her eyes again. 'Actually, I th-think it's all right now. I c-can't feel any burning – come to that, I can't feel anything at all. C-can I come out now, d'you think?'

'Well, I think we might just allow it.' His voice was slow and lazy again, the brisk authority with which he'd dealt with the accident apparently shelved. 'Though you do look enticingly attractive in there with that rather transparent slip on.' He laughed as Felicity glanced down at herself and gave a small gasp of horror. The slip seemed almost to have disappeared, leaving her covered by no more than a couple of wisps of lace which left nothing to anybody's imagination. Least of all an artist's, she thought confusedly. For heaven's sake, how long had he been enjoying this view, while she had her eyes closed? Her skin washed scarlet with embarrassment, she reached out her arms for the towel Jake was holding out.

'Please, Jake. I'm all right, really. There's no burning at all – I'm not even pink, look.' Her confusion grew and Jake laughed again. 'Oh, look, stop fooling about and give me the towel, will you!' she exclaimed, beginning to laugh herself. 'I'm freezing.'

'Try a little bit of running on the spot to

warm yourself up,' he suggested, and held the towel out like a matador's cape. *'Ole!* And it's Jose winning now – no, it's not, it's the bull – Jose – the bull. And the bull's got the cape – he's got Jose – the crowd roars – *Ole, ole, ole!* Now, don't you feel warmer?'

'Jake, you are a fool,' she began, reaching in vain for the towel as he held it tantalisingly near and then whipped it away again. Half-laughing, half-embarrassed, she stretched her arms, twisting her body in an effort to catch the fluttering pink fabric. 'Oh, please, just let me have it!' she exclaimed as he flicked it around her with all the dexterity and panache of a real toreador. 'Please!'

Jake stopped suddenly. Her laughter faded and died. She turned her head slowly, looked over her shoulder, then glanced briefly, eloquently, back at Jake, her heart plummeting. He was quite still, his expression almost totally enigmatic, but somewhere deep in his eyes she detected a flicker of ... what?

There was no time to consider it now. She turned to face the man who stood in the doorway.

'I found your garden door open,' Geoffrey said stiffly. His eyes took in the scene before

129

him as if he were watching some film he couldn't believe in. 'I heard noises – came to see if you were all right.'

Felicity felt the scorch of his gaze, as his eyes raked down her body, more keenly than she had felt the burns from the hot coffee. She opened her mouth to speak but Geoffrey forestalled her.

'Clearly, you are. I'm sorry to have intruded.' He turned on his heel, then added, 'I brought those papers over that we talked about – I'll leave them on your table. Perhaps you'll have time to glance at them sometime when you're not quite so busy.' He flung a glance of contempt and disgust at Jake, swept her once again with the same withering look, and was gone.

In silence, still with that devilish glint in his eyes, Jake held out the towel and Felicity wrapped her almost naked body in it and clutched it around her. She didn't look at him as he followed Geoffrey out of the bathroom. Slowly, she dried herself and emerged into the bedroom to find some dry clothes.

To her astonishment, Jake was there, sitting in the small armchair by the window. He glanced at her, his eyes moving with appreciation over her now completely naked body, and said with approval, 'This is *much* better, Felicity. This is the room I was looking for, the room that tells me all about you. The real room. And you–' He got up slowly, tall, lean and dark, and she felt as if her limbs were paralysed as he came across the room. Helplessly, she looked up at him, meeting his deep brown eyes with her own imploring gaze, feeling her heart thunder in her breast. Her lips parted, but barely a whisper passed between them as Jake smiled down at her, then reached out to enfold her in his arms.

'And you,' he said as he bent his head to hers, 'are the real woman.'

Five

'I don't want to hear about it,' Geoffrey said stiffly. 'There can be only one explanation for what was going on last night, Felicity, and I'd really rather you didn't try to tell me any– Anyway, as you're so fond of telling me, your private life is your own affair and after what I saw in your bathroom, I agree that it had better stay that way. I certainly

131

wouldn't want to be involved.'

He turned away, his whole body rigid with disapproval, and Felicity gazed at him in despair. 'Geoff, if only you'd *listen*.'

'Listen? To what? Lies, lame explanations that couldn't even begin to ring true?' He whipped back to face her. 'Felicity, I thought we were friends. We had an understanding. Those Friday evenings we spent together – I saw them as leading us somewhere.' He bowed his head and his voice dropped. 'I've grown very fond of you, Felicity, and I thought it was the same for you. Evidently, I was wrong.'

'No!' Felicity caught herself up, aware that her anxiety could trap her into saying more than she intended. 'I mean – Geoff, I *am* fond of you. I've enjoyed our Fridays together, and our trips to Bournemouth to see Father. But–'

'But it's been no more to you than that. And the last time you went to Bournemouth, you made it quite clear I wasn't wanted.' His mouth twisted with bitterness. 'That was not long after Ashton appeared on the scene, if I remember rightly.'

'It had nothing to do with Jake,' she said quietly. 'I simply needed a break.'

'And you're going to tell me you never got

together that weekend, the two of you?' he enquired sceptically. 'A strange coincidence that he was away on the very days that you were supposedly visiting your father – especially considering how insistent he'd been that he had to spend as much time as possible around the castle.'

Felicity stared at him. 'That weekend? No, I never saw Jake after Friday afternoon. I don't know what you–' Suddenly, she remembered Jake having told her that he'd gone to the Exeter printing works while she'd been away. Geoffrey obviously hadn't known that, but he'd noticed Jake's absence and perhaps heard that they'd been in the pub, apparently together, and put two and two together, even as early as that. Had he been suspicious of her for all that time? 'Geoff, we weren't together that weekend. Jake went to Exeter, to the printer's. He told me afterwards, and if you don't believe me I'm sure it could be checked, they'd remember him there.'

'Oh.' For a moment, Geoffrey seemed at a loss. He quickly recovered himself. 'Well, be that as it may, it doesn't alter what the two of you were up to when I called in yesterday evening.' His eyes were on her again, still almost unbelieving. 'Felicity, if anyone had told me you could behave like that – well, I just wouldn't have believed it. I thought you had more respect for yourself. Why, I've never even dreamed of suggesting ... anything like that.' His mouth curled distastefully. 'What your father would have said...'

'Let's get a few things straight, Geoff,' Felicity said in a low voice. 'One, Jake and I weren't "up to" anything. We were merely having supper together and I had a slight accident. I poured scalding coffee over myself. Jake acted quickly to save me from being burnt: he put me straight under a cold shower. It was the best thing he could have done – there's no sign now of any burn. If he hadn't done that, I could have been badly scorched.' She paused. 'Two, I have plenty of self-respect and haven't done anything to alter that. Three, as you so rightly implied just now, it really isn't any of your business.'

'And you really expect me to believe that?' he jeered. 'You really expect me to believe that you scalded yourself and the only treatment was to strip you naked and put you into a cold shower? Felicity, you ought to turn your hand to writing fairy tales! Why–'

'I wasn't naked,' she said quickly. 'I still

had my slip on.'

'You were as good as naked. From the brief glimpse I had of you, you might as well have been gift-wrapped in cellophane. Look, Felicity, I'm not a complete innocent. I know some people have somewhat warped inclinations, and it's nothing more than I'd expect of a man of Ashton's type. But you–'

Felicity's temper, which had been quietly simmering during the entire argument, came swiftly and suddenly to the boil. She stood up and faced Geoffrey across her desk. Her eyes were sparking like fireworks, ignited with anger, her soft lips hardened.

'Geoffrey, I've told you the truth. I was scalded and Jake saved me from being badly burned. There was nothing more to it than that.' She bit her lip. It was the truth – as far as it went. At the point at which Geoffrey had interrupted them, there had been no more to it than that.

'And all the cavorting about, the towel-waving, the shouts of *Ole,* all these were part of the treatment?' he demanded with heavy sarcasm. 'You ought to write to the medical journals about that, when you're not too busy with the fairy tales. It seems to be quite a breakthrough.'

Felicity flapped an exasperated hand. 'Oh,

that was just Jake playing the fool. You must know by now what he's like.'

'Not really. But then I haven't had your opportunities, have I? I'm sure you know exactly what he's like.'

There was no mistaking the insinuation in Geoffrey's tone. Felicity stared at him for a long moment. Then, very slowly, she sat down.

'All right, Geoff. I think you've said enough now. In fact, we've probably both said a little too much. Let's drop the subject.' She looked up and her eyes were hard, with a flinty look that was seen only when she was at her most implacable. 'But we'll have to consider one or two other things, won't we? Like your position here.'

'My position? I don't quite understand.'

'No? I'd have thought it was fairly plain. You won't want to go on working with a woman who has so obviously lost your respect. And I'm not sure I want to go on working with a chief accountant who believes me to be a liar.' She looked down and drew some papers across the desk towards her. 'You'd better give some thought to the matter.'

She knew by Geoffrey's stillness that he was staring at her. At last he said in an unbelieving voice, 'Are you telling me I'm dismissed, Felicity?'

'It's not as easy as that, is it?' she said without looking up. 'But I'm rather surprised that the question of dismissal even comes into it. I'd have expected resignation to be more likely.'

'Look, let's not be hasty over this.'

'I never was hasty. It wasn't I who misread the situation and refused to listen to explanations.'

She glanced up to see Geoffrey run a hand through his smooth, pale hair, leaving it looking unwontedly ruffled. Just like Geoffrey himself, she thought with a sudden quirk of inner amusement, and wondered what Jake would have made of all this. No doubt he'd have thought it all wonderful stuff and captured every change of expression with his pencil.

The thought of Jake brought a quiver to her heart. But she pushed away the picture it had conjured up. She couldn't afford to let that into her mind – not yet.

'Felicity.' Geoff's voice had lost its bombastic disapproval and become almost uncertain. 'Look, you don't mean this; you're just speaking out of temper.'

'*I'm* not the one in a temper.'

'All right. I did come in here with all guns firing. I'm sorry about that.' He was trying his little-boy charm now, even though the smile did seem to have some trouble in coming. 'But you can't really blame me, can you? I mean, anyone would have misread that situation. And–'

'It never occurred to you, of course, that you shouldn't have been there?' she remarked.

'Well, yes. You know I'd never intrude on you at home if it wasn't important. Those papers–'

'Could have waited until today. As, in fact, they have.' Felicity tapped the sheaf that lay before her. 'No, Geoffrey, I think you came to my flat last night because you knew, or suspected, that Jake would be with me. Isn't that the truth?'

He stared at her, and she met his eyes with a level gaze. At last, he sighed and shrugged.

'No. That's not why I came, but I won't deny that if I had known, I probably would have come anyway. Yes, the papers were an excuse.' He fiddled with Felicity's telephone. 'Look, if I tell you why I came, will you swear to me that what you've just said – about that bathroom business – is the truth?'

'I've already told you it's the truth. I see no need to swear. If you aren't willing to accept that...'

'All right,' he said. 'I accept it. So, nothing happened between you and Ashton. It was just an exercise in first aid.'

'What you saw in the bathroom was no more than that,' she said steadily. 'And Jake playing the fool once he knew I was all right.'

'We'll say no more about that.' He glanced around a little desperately, and pulled up the chair that Jackie used for dictation. 'I'm sorry, I'm not finding this very easy. Not after all that's been said.'

Felicity waited without speaking, determined not to give Geoffrey any help with whatever he wanted to say.

'The fact of the matter is,' he said, taking refuge in pomposity, 'I came to your flat for a specific purpose. There was something important I wanted to discuss with you. Something I wanted to ask you.'

'Something that couldn't wait until you saw me in the office this morning?'

'It wasn't an office matter. Not entirely, anyway. It was, to some fairly considerable degree, personal.'

Why didn't I ever notice how pompous he

is? Felicity thought. Trying not to let her impatience show, but unwilling to forgive him too easily, she said, 'Do go on, Geoff. It sounds fascinating.'

He shot her an uneasy glance, then looked down at his hands.

'The fact is, Felicity, I intended to propose marriage.'

After all his circumlocution, the bald statement came as a shock. Felicity gazed at him, too surprised to speak. Certainly she had suspected that Geoffrey might be growing fond of her, might even want to develop some kind of relationship – might even, eventually, make a proposal of marriage. But, not being at all sure of her own feelings, she'd been inclined to wait to see if her own fondness grew to match his. If not, she could easily have staved off the possibility of anything more serious if it should have begun to appear likely.

And knowing that Geoffrey, being an accountant, normally moved with all the impetuous haste of a giant tortoise pursuing a disabled lettuce, she'd imagined that there was plenty of time.

'Marriage?' she said faintly. 'But...'

'Come on, Felicity, you must have anticipated this.' He was speaking more confidently now. 'We've been spending Friday evenings together for some time now. I've visited your father twice. And you can't have failed to consider the advantages.'

'The ... advantages?'

'Certainly. Look, we all know how marvellously you've done in pulling this company to its feet after you'd taken over the printing business from your father. It's been nothing short of a miracle. And taking over that packaging firm, to say nothing of the builder's merchant division, and turning the whole lot into Grant Industrial Holdings. You've worked wonders and I'm the first to say so. But you're not always going to want to work like you do now, are you?'

'Aren't I?'

'Well, of course not. You're a woman. You'll want marriage, your own home, babies. And you'll want to know that when you do give up, the business will be safe in hands that you trust.' He waved his own hands as if to draw her attention to their trustworthiness. 'And what better hands than those of your husband?'

Felicity gazed at him.

'Let's get this straight, Geoff. You came to my flat last night to propose that we get married so that I can stay at home and have babies while you take over the business. Is that right? That *is* what you're saying?'

'Well, I wouldn't have put it so baldly as that. I mean, I'd have wrapped it up a little—'

'No doubt. After all, you did come to GIH from a packaging company.' Felicity paused. 'Well, since the subject is now no more than academic—'

'Academic? What do you mean?'

She widened her eyes. 'Well, you're only telling me why you came last night, aren't you? You're not actually making such a proposal now. You wouldn't want to – not after what you saw.'

He flicked his fingers dismissively. 'Oh, that! I thought we'd sorted all that out. You tell me nothing happened, I believe you. I've forgotten about it already.' His pale eyes watched her, still uneasy. 'As far as I'm concerned, nothing's changed.'

'Nothing?'

'Nothing. It didn't happen. A silly misunderstanding, that's all. It's behind us now.' He leaned forward, reaching out his hand and twitching the fingers as if he expected her to put her own into it. 'Come on, Felicity. It'd be a strange thing if we didn't have a little spat now and then, wouldn't it? Not many marriages get by

142

without the odd squabble.'

'Geoffrey, we're not married.'

'No, of course not, but–'

'Nor ever likely to be,' she said gently.

She saw his face darken. His rather full, soft mouth thinned and hardened and a small frown gathered the sandy brows together.

'Now look, Felicity, you haven't even given time to consider–'

'I don't have to. This isn't a business proposition, after all. It's – as you said just now – rather more personal. And I know I don't want to marry you. Or anyone,' she added, trying to soften her words a little.

'Not at the moment, perhaps. I can understand that. You've got all this' – he waved his hand vaguely – 'all you've built up. But as I've already pointed out, Felicity, you're not going to want that for ever. It's not natural for a woman to give up the chance of a home and family. You may not want those things now, but you will and before very long, if I'm any judge. After all, what are you – twenty-seven, twenty-eight? And never had any serious relationship with a man? Well, that's not normal, for a start!' He leaned back in his chair, as if satisfied that he had proved his point.

Felicity bit back the anger that had flared in her again and answered in the same quiet voice.

'As it happens, Geoffrey, you're wrong there. I have had serious relationships. One when I was at university, and another shortly afterwards. Neither of them worked out, primarily because neither of them could tolerate the idea of my having a career that was as important to me as theirs was to them.' She paused. 'You may very well be right, that one day I may want to give it all up in favour of a home and children. But if that ever does happen, it will be because I've met a man who can convince me that it's worthwhile. And so far, that hasn't happened.' Her voice quivered a little as she spoke the last words, but within seconds she had it under control again. 'It hasn't happened,' she repeated firmly.

Geoffrey gave her an unexpectedly shrewd glance.

'Are you sure you're not trying to convince yourself as well as me? I'm not well up in Shakespeare, Felicity, but didn't he have some remark to make about a lady who protested too much?' He shook his head. 'Look, we won't discuss it any more now. It's come as a surprise to you, I can see that, though I'd have thought you knew what I've been leading up to, all these Fridays. So–'

'Geoff, please stop talking about a few Friday evenings as if they were an old-fashioned courtship ritual. We went out for the odd meal, saw a film or two, a show – that's all there was to it. I enjoyed them, but I never saw them as a prelude to anything more.' That wasn't strictly true, but she hurried on. 'Look, I'm sorry to have to repeat this, but it's no good. I don't want to marry you. And I shan't change my mind, so please don't ask me again. It'll only hurt you and embarrass us both!'

She met his eyes pleadingly, and saw that he was rejecting her words even as she spoke them. Oh Lord, she thought despairingly, what did I do to deserve this? The last thing I need is a love-sick chief accountant.

Although even now, she wasn't convinced that Geoffrey's proposal had much to do with love. Feeling guilty about her own cynicism, she thought it was far more likely that he saw it as a sound business move.

'It's Ashton, isn't it,' he said abruptly, and Felicity felt a hot tide of colour surge into her cheeks. 'Yes, I can see it is.'

'I don't know what you mean,' she protested. 'You can see nothing of the sort.'

'I can see you blushing,' he retorted. 'What more do I need?'

'You took me by surprise. And after your reaction to what happened last night–'

'Yes, I said we'd forget that, didn't I?' he mused. 'But maybe that wasn't such a good idea. And now I come to think of it, you were a bit evasive over that, weren't you? Oh, willing enough to say that nothing was happening when I came in and caught you. But you haven't said much about what might have happened afterwards. Maybe that's not so easy to cover up, hm?'

Felicity lowered her eyes. Her cheeks stung with the heat of her blood, and she knew that Geoffrey's eyes were on her, missing nothing. No, she hadn't said anything about what had happened after he had left, after she had dried herself and come naked out of the bathroom to find Jake waiting for her. Nor did she intend to.

'I thought so,' Geoffrey said at last, and rose to his feet. 'Well, there's no more to be said, is there? Except, perhaps, two things.' He paused, but Felicity did not look up. 'You might like to consider them both. One is that Jake Ashton isn't all he seems – I've been making the odd enquiry. You might like to ask him how well he knows Sir

Michael Butterford, sometime when you're not too busy. And while you're at it, ask him why he's really been so keen to spend time in your office. It's not for the purposes of this painting, I'm ready to swear. And I don't think he's the man to pass up the chance of making a little extra money for himself, from a spot of industrial espionage.'

Felicity lifted her head quickly, opening her mouth to speak, but Geoffrey continued, 'That's one thing you might like to think about. And the other is this – just what would your Board think if they knew what had been going on in your flat last night? Not that I'd dream of telling them, of course. After all, a man wouldn't want those sort of stories circulating about his wife ... would he?'

He turned away before Felicity could gather words together for a reply, pausing only with his hand on the doorknob, where he turned to give her a bland smile.

'That's blackmail,' she whispered. 'You wouldn't...?'

'Wouldn't I?' Geoffrey said pleasantly. 'Care to try me?'

Left alone, Felicity dropped her head into her hands. The scene with Geoffrey had left her shaken and upset. She needed coffee, but dared not ring through to Jackie until she was sure she had command of herself. She sat quite still, fighting the emotions that surged within her, Geoffrey's words circling like vicious insects in her brain.

Why had she never seen before what kind of man he was? Why had she never realised how jealous he was of her position, how anxious to step into her shoes?

But it wasn't only the threats he had made against her that hammered in her mind. It was what he had said about Jake. That remark about industrial espionage – it must surely have been a spiteful shot in the dark, made without foundation. But what did Geoffrey mean about him and Sir Michael? Could there really be anything sinister there?

She shook her head. Thinking about Jake only brought back even more forcibly the events of the previous evening. And those had been seared in her brain for all time. She let them come flooding in again now, from the moment when she had emerged from the bathroom and Jake had come to her, taken her in his arms and said she was the woman he'd been waiting for...

'Jake,' she'd protested nervously, burningly aware of her nakedness under his cool hands and against his thin shirt. 'Jake, please – let me get dressed.'

'When you're so beautiful as you are? Don't tell me you're still cold.' His eyes laughed down at her and she stared into them, bemused by the dancing flecks of gold, the sparkling warmth. 'Don't you think I deserve a little reward for saving you from burning?' he added teasingly.

Felicity shook her head. 'Jake, stop fooling about and let me go.' The words came almost automatically, like a conditioned response, the response of any woman who found herself naked in the arms of a man she scarcely knew. But on a deeper level, she was aware of a response that was quite different – the response of a primitive and vital being who knew very well the arms that held her, the body that pressed so intimately against hers. And who liked it – wanted more of it. Her heart thundered suddenly in her breast, her blood roared in her ears, and she trembled against him.

'Jake!' she said again, and her voice was edged with panic. 'Please – let me go!'

At once, his arms loosened, though he still held her lightly in their circle. His eyes were grave now, searching her face, and she felt a weakness creep through her body, a warm langour that softened and parted her lips as she gazed up at him. Without thinking, she let her own hands rest against his shoulders, and felt his palms touch gently, burningly, against her shoulder blades.

'Don't be afraid,' he said in a voice that seemed to be made of softest cashmere. 'You've no cause to be afraid of me, Felicity.'

'Are you sure?' she breathed, and he shook his head slowly.

'To be honest – no, I'm not sure.' For an instant, his old impishness danced in his eyes. 'I ought to be, for God's sake. I've seen and painted enough naked women in my time. But you – you, Felicity, are something else. A woman apart.' She was paralysingly conscious of those fingers, just touching her shoulder blades, tracing the silkiness of the skin over the edge of bone, caressing, circling. 'The woman,' he said again in husky tones, 'that I've been waiting for.'

'What do you mean?' she whispered.

'I mean that ever since I first met you, I've been conscious that underneath that brisk, efficient exterior there was a real woman struggling to get out. You hid her well,

Felicity, but not well enough for me. I knew she was there, right from the start.'

His hands crossed over her back and she felt his fingers slip under her arms, perilously close to the sensitive tissue of her breasts. Nervously, she moved a little, then shivered. At once, his eyes sharpened.

'You're not still cold?'

'No,' she murmured, and her glance fell beneath his penetrating scrutiny. 'No, I'm not cold.'

He gathered her a little closer. 'Mind you,' he went on conversationally, 'the real Felicity's got a lot of struggling to do yet, before she finally escapes. What happened just now gave her no more than a glimpse of freedom. But even that might be enough to give her a taste for it. I hope so anyway.' Felicity looked up again and met his eyes, amused now though there was a serious intentness lurking somewhere deep in those forest pools. 'And you're not doing so badly even now, are you? I wonder just what you'd have said if I'd told you earlier that you'd be standing here in my arms, naked as the day your mother bore you.'

'Jake!' She stared at him. 'You *meant* this to happen! Oh, you – you–'

'Easy, now, easy!' Laughing openly now,

he caught her flailing fists and held her firmly. 'How could I have engineered that little accident? I didn't arrange for your wrist to be weak or the coffee pot too heavy. I certainly wouldn't have risked your being scalded. No, once you'd spilled that coffee, everything else that happened was inevitable. Except, perhaps, for that rather untimely interruption.'

'Oh, yes.' Diverted, she allowed herself to be gathered close again. 'Geoffrey. How on earth am I going to explain to him? He'll never believe the truth.'

'And you certainly won't want to tell him lies.' Jake shrugged, unconcerned. 'Nothing you can do about him, I'd say. Just let him stew in his own buttoned-up, disapproving juice.'

'It's all very well for you,' she protested, half-laughing. 'But I have to work with him. I shan't be able to look him in the face.'

'Another good thing to have come out of this evening's events,' he remarked, and Felicity laughed in spite of herself.

'Jake, you're impossible!'

'A little unlikely, perhaps,' he acknowledged. 'But not impossible. You know, you really are extremely pleasant to hold, Felicity. Do you mind if I kiss you?'

Startled, she looked up at him. It seemed, in the circumstances, to be a superfluous question, but Jake seemed to be quite serious and she found herself reacting almost as a young girl might react to her first kiss.

'Well – I suppose not,' she stammered, once more aware of those circling fingers, moving now somewhere around the small of her back, gently subtle, barely touching the skin that almost stood up in an effort to reach them. And, acutely conscious of what it might lead to, she lifted her face, lips slightly parted.

Jake bent his head, his beard brushing her cheek with unexpected softness, and laid his mouth against hers. She felt his lips firm and insistent, shaping hers; felt her mouth open to his will as his tongue made a tender but decisive entry. For a brief moment, she fought against it, but Jake's hands were implacable now, holding her close enough to feel the rapid beat of his heart. One slid up her back to spread long, sensitive fingers through her dark, wet hair and clasp her head, the other slipped under her arm again – an arm that had somehow, with its twin, reached up to wind itself around Jake's neck – and stroked the edge of her breast with a softly-moving thumb.

Felicity, caught in a kiss which seemed to have no end, moaned softly in her throat and shifted against him, straining to hold her body closer still. Her heart was hammering wildly, her skin on fire under his touch. She wasn't even sure whether she was breathing or not. The brisk, no-nonsense business-woman, the Felicity who had built up an industrial company from a failing printing works, had disappeared, her few feeble protests lost and forgotten in the tumult of feeling and desire that swept through her like a firestorm, threatening to devour both herself and Jake in an emotional holocaust of an intensity she had never imagined possible.

Jake ended the kiss at last with a minute peck at the corner of her mouth. Breathing quickly, he let his lips move over her face, touching her cheeks and eyelids, nibbling at the lobes of her ears. He was holding her with one arm around her shoulders now, his strength more than compensating for the weakness of her trembling legs, and with his other hand he cupped her breast, his fingertips exploring with exquisite sensitivity, taking her nipple between thumb and forefinger to exert the slightest of pinching movements on its erect hardness. His mouth leaving her face at last, he dropped his head, stroked the springing curls of beard down the column of her neck, and planted a kiss as light as a falling blossom on the swollen flesh. Then he lifted himself upright again and drew her close, holding her almost as if to comfort her.

'Jake...' she breathed, when she had found her voice again. 'Oh ... Jake...'

'I told you I knew there was a woman in there somewhere,' he muttered. 'And what a woman! Felicity – you're dynamite. So much so–' His voice was husky, deep in his throat, the words almost lost. His hands tightened on her body, the fingers moving almost convulsively over skin that burned all over again. Then, as if with an effort, he moved a little away from her and surveyed her with dark eyes that kindled with desire. 'So much so that we're going to stop right there. Enough's enough for a first time.'

'I – I don't understand,' Felicity stammered, and he laughed softly, a little shakily.

'It's easy, Felicity. You have your wish – you may get dressed now.' His eyes moved over her trembling body, dark and unfathomable. 'I believe you *are* cold, you know,' he said gently.

'But don't you want—'

'To kiss you again? To take you into that delectable bed, in this bedroom which tells me so much about you?' His glance left hers for a moment to rove about the room with its softly-coloured furnishings, its pale gold carpet and flowered bedcover. 'My God, Felicity, do you have to ask? There's nothing I'd like better! But not now. Not tonight.'

He stepped closer again but did not take her into his arms. Instead, he lifted one hand and touched her cheek with a finger. Instinctively, Felicity turned her cheek into his palm, and heard a soft murmur, almost a growl, deep within his chest.

'I want to give the real Felicity time to come out of hiding,' he said quietly. 'Time to find herself. Then – we'll see. Meanwhile—' and now he had command of himself again, his mouth twitching, eyes crinkling in the grin that had so maddened and infuriated her, even while she'd been unable to help laughing '—meanwhile, I'm going to paint one hell of a good picture!'

He gave her a final, long look, then turned and went out of the bedroom. And Felicity, standing alone and shivering in the middle of the carpet, heard the garden door close as he let himself out.

By the time she forced herself to move, she was really cold, her shivers caused now by the chill of approaching night. Slowly, stiffly, she opened the wardrobe and took out a soft wrap, drawing it around her like a blanket. She sank down on the bed and stared out at the darkened garden.

Had he really been thinking only of his picture when he had held and kissed her in an attempt to set the 'real Felicity' free? Had it meant no more to him than that?

Had the feel of her in his arms, her skin naked against his body, been nothing more than 'extremely pleasant'?

If so, it was nothing short of cruelty. Because by waking the 'real Felicity' he had set free a clamouring, wild, primitive being who was already making her presence felt, tearing with nails and teeth at her prison, determined to escape and take what must be rightfully hers. A being who threatened to create havoc in the old Felicity, the brisk, efficient business girl, company chairman and managing director who had been beaten by no man and now seemed doomed to be beaten by her own unsuspected self.

Six

Towards the middle of the afternoon, Felicity pressed the switch on her intercom. When Jackie answered, she said in a tone that tried hard to be casual, 'I haven't seen Jake today, Jackie. Is he coming in, d'you know?'

Her secretary's voice sounded faintly surprised as she replied.

'Why, no, Miss Grant. Surely he must have told you? He says he's finished working in your office. Got all the atmosphere he needs, apparently. He'll be using the studio from now on, when he's not observing the other Board members.'

'Oh,' Felicity said blankly. 'Yes, of course, he did mention it – I'd forgotten. Sorry to have disturbed you, Jackie.'

'That's all right, Miss Grant. Seems odd without him around, doesn't it?' the disembodied voice remarked. 'I know he hadn't been coming in long, really, but I'd got used to him being about. He brightened the place up.'

'Yes, he did.' Felicity hesitated. 'So he's in the studio now, is he?'

'No, not today. Told me he was taking a couple of days' break before he starts the next stage. I don't quite know when he'll be in again.'

'I see. All right, Jackie, thanks.' Felicity switched off again, feeling oddly deflated. Ever since arriving that morning, she'd been on edge, half-dreading, half-longing for Jake's appearance. Now, it seemed that he wasn't coming in at all – perhaps for several days. And he hadn't even bothered to let her know.

Resentment prickled in her mind. Just what was he playing at? Giving her all that tale about his search for the 'real woman' inside her. Engineering that very intimate scene in her bedroom, at the memory of which her cheeks still burned – and if he hadn't arranged for her to be scalded, he'd certainly waited for her to come naked out of that shower. If the accident with the coffee hadn't happened, she had no doubt he'd have found some other way of getting her into his arms. And of kissing her the way he had, so that even now, seventeen and a half hours later, her heart still quivered with remembered emotion.

And after all that, he'd just left her. Flat. Hadn't come to the office. Hadn't even rung up to say hello, or goodbye. Restlessly, she pushed at the pens that lay across her desk and glanced across at the corner where Jake normally sat. It looked strangely empty.

This wouldn't do! And with the quarrel with Geoffrey still rankling, she reached for the telephone. His threats she had dismissed as being no more than the angry blows of a child, hitting out in a temper tantrum. But she couldn't have her chief accountant behaving like a thwarted toddler. They would have to discuss the matter again, more reasonably. Perhaps by now he would have cooled down.

'I'm sorry, Miss Grant,' Geoffrey's secretary said, 'he's not here. He's gone to Exeter. I don't think he expected to be back this afternoon. But you could catch him there.'

'No, it's not that important.' Felicity replaced the telephone and tapped her fingers on her desk for a moment or two. Then she straightened her shoulders and pulled the Haverford file towards her. There was plenty of work to be done on this, especially in view of the talk she'd had with Sir Michael Butterford. And that thought brought her straight back to Geoffrey – and Jake. Just what had Geoffrey meant by his remark? And how well *did* Jake and Sir Michael know each other?

Industrial espionage. They'd never had an instance of it in Grant Holdings. But that didn't mean it couldn't happen. And Jake *had* been in an ideal position to see and hear things that were normally treated as confidential.

No. It was nonsense.

All the same...

The intercom on her desk buzzed and Jackie said, 'It's Mr Earnshaw to see you, Miss Grant. Shall I send him in?'

'Yes, I'm free at present.' Felicity stifled a groan. Nigel Earnshaw was her least favourite member of the Board, though she had to admit that he was efficient. Almost too efficient, she thought wryly, remembering that she had suspected him of wanting to step into her own shoes. And with his qualifications, both in law and printing administration, together with his background of experience both with a large printing firm in London and an electronics engineering company, he would be well able to do just that, should the Board ever decide that Felicity wasn't up to the job any more.

Wondering what he wanted, Felicity closed the file she had just opened and looked up.

Nigel Earnshaw came in. He was just forty, old enough to look on Felicity as a 'girl' and rarely missing an opportunity to say so. He had been managing director of the packaging firm Grant Holdings had bought out just before her father had retired and, evidently not appreciating the extent of Felicity's involvement at that time, could well have expected to take over the newly expanded company. Instead, he had been made responsible for their own packaging department. He had never displayed any resentment, but Felicity was uncomfortably sure it was there, lurking like a rock beneath deceptively smooth waters.

He was tall, with a long thin face and straight, smooth black hair combed back uncompromisingly from his forehead. His eyes reminded Felicity of prunes, swimming in slightly yellowed juice, and the colour of his teeth echoed the impression of sourness. Until Felicity banned all tobacco from her office and Board meetings, he had filled the air with acrid smoke, and his fingertips betrayed that he was still heavily addicted to nicotine. Nevertheless, he did his job efficiently and sometimes brilliantly, and Felicity could not deny that he was a valuable Board member.

'Hallo, Nigel,' she said with a friendly smile. 'Sit down. Nice to see you. Is there anything special, or is this just a social call?'

'I don't make social calls,' Nigel said, with perfect truth. He was the least sociable of all the Board members. At least he never wasted time on small talk. With Nigel, you were always sure of coming straight to the point. 'Look,' he said, 'I want to talk to you about this Ashton character. He's been snooping about.'

'Snooping about?' Felicity repeated, startled. 'Oh, I don't think so, Nigel. He's just working on this picture of his. I admit his method of working isn't very conventional – but then, what is conventional for an artist? He's just getting atmosphere, that's all.'

'He seems to think he can wander in and out of all our offices at will. He was hanging around me all lunchtime last Friday. I found it damned distracting, I don't mind telling you.'

'Well, he did say he wanted to spend time with all the Board members,' Felicity pointed out. 'Perhaps Friday lunchtime was the only chance he had.'

'It was the only chance *I* had to get a bit of work done in peace,' Nigel grumbled. 'Instead of which, I had the Ghost of Christmas Yet to Come hanging over me, watching my every move. It's nothing to laugh at, Felicity! Apart from anything else–'

'I'm sorry,' she said, controlling her amusement. 'It was just the expression you used. And really, you don't have anything to complain about, Nigel. He spent days and days in here. I thought he was never going to go.'

'Knew when he was on to a cushy number, that's why.' Nigel still sounded aggrieved. 'Apart from anything else, Felicity, there's a definite security risk. The man could hear anything. He's probably picked up no end of confidential information. And he may be an artist, but he's not a fool.'

Felicity frowned. 'Are you saying he might be a spy?'

'I don't know what he is. I just think there's a risk.' Nigel paused for a moment, then added more decisively, 'Yes, I do think he could be a spy. And that brings me to my second reason for coming to see you.'

'Your second reason?' Felicity's heart sank.

'Yes. The Haverford contract.' Nigel's eyes lit on the file on Felicity's desk. 'I see you're working on it yourself now.'

'Yes. Sir Michael Butterford came to see me—'

'And?'

'I was going to bring it up at the next Board meeting,' Felicity said, irritated to hear a defensive note in her voice. 'It's all very tentative at present, but—'

'There's a chance of a takeover, isn't there?' Nigel said bluntly.

Felicity was silent for a moment. Then, quietly, she said, 'Yes. A very slight chance. I'm not even worrying about it. I think they're just kite-flying. But—'

'But it's there,' he persisted, and she sighed.

'Yes. It's there.'

Nigel stared at her for a moment. Automatically, his fingers reached into his pocket for his cigarettes, then he remembered and withdrew them again. He drew in his lips and drummed his fingers on the arm of his chair.

'Don't you think this warranted a special Board meeting?'

Felicity lifted her head. Her eyes sparked a little.

'No, I don't. Or I'd have called one. Nigel, it's no more than a whisper. When Sir Michael came here–'

'He was spying out the land. Didn't you realise that? Felicity, a whisper's all it needs to send rumours flying on the Stock Exchange. And if we have someone who hasn't got the company's interests at heart, poking and prying around the offices hearing God knows what and putting his own interpretation on it, there's no knowing what might happen.'

'I'm sure Jake–'

'You're *not* sure, Felicity. You can't be. Unless the man's been positive-vetted, and we don't have the means to do that.'

'Oh, Nigel, don't you think you're taking all this a bit too seriously? He's a painter. He's not interested in anything besides his picture.' As I could tell you only too well, she thought bitterly. 'Look, I really think you're over-reacting about this. But just in case you're not, I'll keep you posted about Sir Michael and the Haverford contract. Meanwhile, I think Jake's just about finished in the offices. He'll be working in his own studio from now on, so there'll be nothing further to worry about,'

'Let's hope you're right,' Nigel said, getting to his feet. 'Furthermore, let's hope it's not too late already. Someone, somewhere, may be preparing at this very moment to sit behind that very nice desk of yours, Felicity.'

He gave her a brief nod and stalked from the room, leaving a distinct aroma of tobacco behind him. Even when he didn't smoke, he carried the aura with him. Felicity watched him go, then got up automatically to open another window.

If anyone was preparing to sit at her desk, she thought, it wasn't Sir Michael Butterford. It was much more likely to be Nigel Earnshaw himself.

The next two days passed quietly. There was no word from Jake, and Felicity tried hard to tell herself she was thankful. Nonetheless, she found herself glancing far too often at the corner where he had ensconced himself, with his large sheets of sketch-paper spread before him, and it seemed lonely drinking coffee without him. She took to wandering out to share her pot with Jackie when she had no visitors, talking to her secretary more than she ever had before. As if they were friends, rather than employer and employee.

It struck her then that she really hadn't got many friends. Those she had made at university were mostly in other parts of the country, or even abroad. And the only member of the Board that she'd allowed to come close to her had been Geoffrey, who was still maintaining a sulky silence.

'Have you heard from Jake lately?' Jackie asked one afternoon as they drank tea together. 'He hasn't been in at all to that studio you set up for him. Seems funny – but perhaps he's got some other job that needs doing.'

'I should hope not,' Felicity said with some indignation. 'He's supposed to be working for us, not gallivanting off on other jobs. I took it that he was working at home for a while.'

'Could be, I suppose. Mind, if I lived where he does I wouldn't want to leave it just now. Must be lovely up there at this time of year. Not that it isn't beautiful here at Stallymore, of course, but that part seems special, somehow.'

'I don't actually know where he does live,' Felicity said after a moment. 'Have you been to his home, Jackie?'

'Oh, no. They say he never invites anyone there. But you know where it is, Miss Grant – at the top of Chillacombe Lane, leading on to the moor out of the village. Off the Widecombe road,' she added, seeing that Felicity still looked mystified. 'Well, I'm not surprised you don't know it really. It's like a hidden village there. The road's a dead end, you see, so if you weren't going there for a purpose you wouldn't know it even existed. And the lane Jake lives up – well, it's more of a track really, it only goes to his cottage. And there's a kind of little wood all around, and a stream running through the garden off the moor – it really is lovely.'

'You seem to know it very well, for someone who's never been there,' Felicity remarked dryly, but Jackie only smiled.

'My auntie lives there. She's known Jake since he was a little boy.'

'Yes, he told me he'd lived here years ago. I'm surprised we never ran across each other before. I used to come here a lot when I was a child, you know, and I knew a lot of the local children then. And with my cousin Andrew knowing him ... well, he's nine or ten years older than me, so I suppose it's natural that our paths never crossed.' Felicity set down her cup. 'That was a nice cup of tea, Jackie, thanks. I'll get back to work. I've got to make arrangements about that shipment of corned beef.' And she went back to her office, a small smile tugging at her lips as she remembered Jake's incredulity at the 'barter' system of trading he had discovered.

She worked on until six, enjoying the quiet after the office staff had gone home and no more phone calls were likely to come through. At last she had done all that she could for that day and she threw down her pen, switched off the dictating machine, swivelled her chair to face the tall windows and stretched luxuriously.

'That's a very pretty sight.'

Felicity gasped and spun her chair back to face the door. Jake Ashton was standing just inside, his dark eyes surveying her, his tousled hair, yellow neckerchief and bright green waistcoat making him look more like a gypsy than ever.

'*Jake!*' Try as she might to prevent it, Felicity felt a wide, idiotic grin spread across her face. 'Where did you spring from?'

'The star-trap in the floor, of course, like all good demons.' He came in and closed the door behind him. 'Pleased to see me?'

'Not in the least,' she told him severely. 'In

fact, we were all celebrating the fact that you seemed to have abandoned us. Where have you been, Jake?'

'Oh, here and there, here and there.' He sauntered over to her desk. 'You're not the only one who's busy, you know. I had important work to attend to.'

'The picture?'

'The picture?' he said, as if he had never heard of it. 'Oh, no. Other work. Something that couldn't be put off.'

'As our picture obviously could,' she said coolly, her grin under control now. Really, just who did he think he was, abandoning her for days and then wandering in as if he owned the place? 'Jake, who let you in? The main door's supposed to be locked once everyone's gone.'

'It is. I've been here about an hour. Came in before the others had packed up.' He settled himself on a corner of her desk and picked up a pencil and a sheet of paper. 'Is this scrap? I've been in that very nice little studio you were kind enough to set up for me.'

'Oh.' Felicity looked at him. So he'd been here an hour, presumably without anyone's knowledge. 'You – you've been in the studio all that time?'

'Most of it, yes. Had a little wander round, once everything was quiet. This really is a very nice castle, Felicity – I do think you ought to open it up a bit to other people.'

'We've discussed that before. It's not on.' Uneasily, she watched the pencil drive strong lines across the paper. 'Jake, when you say you had a wander round–'

'I mean just that. I wandered round. Why? You've no objection, have you?' He gave her a bright glance. 'If I can do it during the day, when there are people about, why not after they've all gone home?'

'No reason.' But she couldn't help remembering Geoffrey's insinuations, and Nigel's warning. 'Jake, how well d'you know Sir Michael Butterford?'

'Mike Butterford? Pretty well, I suppose. His daughter's a friend of mine. Owns that gallery in Exeter. Remember, we met in the new restaurant the night it opened? Fiona was very taken with the idea of my painting a lady tycoon.'

'Fiona? That was Fiona Butterford? The one who's always being photographed for the society pages? Sir Michael's daughter?'

'That's right. Haven't you ever met her?'

'No,' Felicity said faintly. 'I – I only know Sir Michael through business.'

'Oh, I'll have to introduce you sometime. You'd probably get on well together. Fiona's a great girl.' He finished his sketch and tossed it down in front of her. Slightly bemused, Felicity picked it up and saw a bitingly accurate caricature of Geoffrey, looking exactly like the large white bull she had pictured herself, with blunted horns, a ring through his nose and a baffled expression. Involuntarily, she laughed.

'Jake, this is really cruel! But it's just like him. Except – well, there's something about his eyes I'm not quite sure of.'

'There is, isn't there,' Jake agreed. He lifted himself from her desk. 'You can keep it if you like. Maybe if you look a bit harder, you'll be able to see what it is.'

'I'll have to be careful he never sees it,' she said, still smiling. 'He'd be absolutely livid. You know, Jake, you've got a real talent for this. Have you ever thought of doing it professionally?'

'I am an artist,' he reminded her dryly and she blushed.

'I know. I meant cartoons.' She looked up at him in mock horror. 'I hope you're not going to turn the Board picture into a giant caricature, are you?'

'But of course,' he said. 'Isn't that what

you wanted? Geoffrey as a bull. Your cousin Andrew as a goat, with that thin beard he insists on wearing. Nigel Earnshaw as a worn-out racehorse. John Ferguson as a – let's see–'

'Stop it,' she begged. 'I'm terrified you'll really do it. And no, I don't want to hear how you'd picture me. Oh, Jake, it *is* good to see you again.' The words slipped out before she knew they were even in her mind. She caught her breath, remembering how they had parted on the last occasion they had been together. Jake the one in command; herself reduced to a quivering jelly. Her face burning, she looked down at her desk.

'And they say the modern woman doesn't know how to blush,' Jake said quietly. 'Do you have any idea just how enchanting you look, Felicity?'

She raised her eyes. He was leaning on the desk, his face close to hers, his eyes intent. He moved to rest his elbows on the polished wood and cupped her chin in his hands. His lips came close and brushed hers to and fro, very gently, before parting them for his kiss.

Felicity lifted her own hands and laid them on his shoulders. Her fingers tightened on the muscles beneath the fabric of his shirt. She felt her heart quiver and leap like a salmon coming upstream; then her whole attention was concentrated on the kiss as she savoured every tiny movement, every thrust of his tongue, every gentle yet insistent alteration in the shape his mouth was making of hers.

'She's still there,' he murmured at last. 'The real Felicity. She's still there, just under the surface. I was half afraid she might have gone back into hiding.'

'I don't know who I am any more,' she whispered, and he chuckled.

'You don't need to. I know who you are, and I'll bring you out into the sunlight. You've stayed in the shadows too long.' He paused for a brief moment. 'It'll be like coming out from under the trees to find a secret, sunlit pool.'

Felicity jerked her head up in astonishment. What did he know of that – the hidden lake? But before she could ask him, before she could even begin to shape the words, the quiet air was split by the sudden ring of the telephone. The unexpectedness of it made her jump violently, and then she stared at the instrument with a mixture of indignation and dismay.

'Well, aren't you going to answer it?' Jake asked in amusement.

'I don't know who it can be,' she said, bewildered. 'Surely nobody would ring the office at this hour. Everyone knows the staff goes home at five thirty.'

'So perhaps it's someone trying to contact you,' he pointed out. 'Presumably everyone also knows that it doesn't make history when you work late. In any case, there's only one way to find out.'

Felicity nodded slowly. The telephone was still ringing and she stretched out her hand to pick it up, suddenly convinced it was Geoffrey. Perhaps he had seen Jake in the building and was checking to see whether they were together. Well, if he were, she'd have great delight in telling him.

'Hello? Grant Industrial Holdings,' she said cautiously.

'Oh, Felicity, thank goodness,' said a woman's voice. 'I've been ringing the flat. I was afraid you'd gone out and then it struck me that you were probably still working. My dear–'

'Peggy?' At the sound of the voice of her father's housekeeper, Felicity's senses sharpened. 'Is something wrong? Dad?'

'He's had a small heart attack, dear. They say it's not serious, but I think he'd like to see you. He told me not to bother you, but you know what he's like. Do you think you could come?'

'Of course. I'll come straight away. Where is he? In hospital?'

'In the Infirmary. They took him there to be on the safe side. You know where it is, don't you? He's in Ward D.'

'Ward D. You're there now, are you?'

'Yes. I'll stay till you come.'

'All right, Peggy. Thanks. I'll see you as soon as possible.' Felicity rang off and looked up at Jake. 'It's my father. He's had a heart attack – small, Peggy says, but they've taken him to hospital. I must go at once.' Half-way to her feet, she remembered something. 'Oh, no! My car's in dock. And it'll be too late even to hire one now. Oh God!'

'We'll go in mine,' Jake said at once. 'You can't drive all that way alone anyway, not while you're worrying about your father. It's all right,' he added, seeing her about to protest. 'I'm a free agent, remember? I can come and go as I please. Nobody's going to raise their eyebrows if I don't come home for a day or two.'

'But you can't just drop everything and go to Bournemouth. In any case, I may need to stay on.'

'Then I can stay on too,' he said cheerfully. 'You may be glad to have someone on hand to use as errand boy. Or I could come back and pick up your car for you. There's no end to the uses I can be put to.' His eyes grew serious again and he laid a strong, sensitive hand on Felicity's shoulder. 'Don't waste time arguing, Felicity. The important thing is to get you there as quickly as we possibly can. We can worry about the logistics of it afterwards. Now, run along to your flat and pack whatever you need for a few days' stay, just in case. As it happens, I've still got my own bag in my car so I don't need to go home. I'll tidy up here.'

'But those files – they have to be put in the safe.' She hesitated, looking at the muddle on her desk. 'And the papers for the Haverford contract–'

'I'll see to everything. I think I can understand enough to put the right papers in the right files, and closing the safe is a simple matter – I've watched you do it often enough.' He pushed her firmly towards the door. 'Go along, Felicity – hurry. Your father's waiting for you.'

Felicity paused only long enough to give him a grateful smile, then ran out of the door and along the corridor to her flat.

Thank goodness Jake had been with her when the call came through, she thought, cramming a few clothes into a suitcase. And thank goodness he was the kind of person he was.

Geoffrey would, of course, have been equally anxious to help. But Geoffrey's help was too often crowded with fussing about detail. He would never have let her go off without tidying her own desk. And he would have wanted to go home, to pack a neat suitcase with whatever clothes might be suitable for any occasion he was likely to encounter.

Felicity shivered as she thought what one of those occasions might be. Oh no, please, no, she prayed. Not yet. Don't let him die yet. I'm not ready.

Not ready to be left alone.

The journey seemed endless. Jake drove his five-year-old car smoothly and efficiently, with none of the erratic showiness she had half feared. In fact, in contrast with Geoffrey, he was totally without aggression towards other road users and the journey was in consequence much less fraying to the nerves than any outing with Geoffrey was inclined to be. As he drove, he asked questions about her father, as if sensing that she wanted to talk about him.

'He started the printing firm, didn't he? The one Grant Holdings began with?'

'Well, he took it over from my grandfather after the war. It was only tiny then, but quite flourishing during the fifties and sixties. Then the recession started and like a lot of other small businesses, it began to fail. By the time I'd finished university, he was about to sell up. I just managed to persuade him to let me come in. He was very reluctant, saw me wasting my opportunities. But – well, we pulled through, expanded into other markets and the rest, as they say, is history.'

'You make it all sound very easy,' he observed, and Felicity smiled and shook her head.

'It wasn't. It was a lot of hard work. And I had trouble persuading Dad to retire. Then he had his first heart attack and saw the light. He retired to Bournemouth and found Peggy to look after him and everything's worked out well.'

'Peggy's his housekeeper?'

'Well, rather more than that now. Oh, I don't mean there's anything between them – but they're friends now, rather than employer and employee. Peggy's a real treasure and a nice woman. He could do a lot worse than marry her,' she added thoughtfully.

'Tell me,' he said after a short silence, 'what made you come back to Stallymore?'

Felicity turned and looked at him. There was something in the tone of his voice that told her his question was not so casual as it seemed. 'Why, I thought I'd told you that before. I used to come here for holidays as a child. My grandfather lived here then, my mother's father. All the children in the family came – Andrew and all my other cousins. It was neglected even then; Grandad didn't have the money to keep it going. When he died, Andrew inherited it but he wanted to work abroad in civil engineering – well, you know that – and wasn't interested in maintaining it. I was just beginning to make quite a lot of money and wanted a headquarters, somewhere out of town – so we made a deal. Andrew let me have the place for a song and I gave him a place on the Board. And since he's highly experienced in building and has a lot of foreign contacts, I think we got the best of both worlds.'

'And Stallymore means no more to you than that?' Jake asked quietly. 'A derelict house, going for a song and with a valuable Board member thrown in? With maybe just a touch of nostalgia?'

Felicity opened her mouth to refute his words indignantly, then paused. Why did she need to do that? Why did she need to justify herself to this man at all?

And could his words actually be true?

'No,' she said after a long, thoughtful moment. 'Stallymore doesn't mean just that. It means more, much more. But' – she turned and faced him with honesty, her grey eyes candid as a child's – 'I'm not quite sure what it does mean. I've never really taken the time to think about it deeply enough.'

'No,' he said as they began to run through the outskirts of Bournemouth. 'I thought that might be the case. May I suggest, then, that you do take that time, sometime soon? It could be important. And now we ought to be nearly at the hospital. Can you direct me, Felicity?'

With a suddenly beating heart, she turned her attention to the streets. It was almost three hours since Peggy's phone call. Almost anything could have happened in the meantime.

She nerved herself for whatever was to come.

Seven

As they approached the door of Ward D, a woman got up from a seat by the wall and came towards them. Her face was pale with anxiety, but she was quite composed and answered Felicity's cry of recognition with a smile.

'Peggy! Oh, thank goodness you're here. How – how is he?'

'The doctor's with him now. I should think he'll be out soon. He'll be able to tell you more than I can.' Peggy's eyes moved to Jake.

'Oh, this is Jake Ashton. He brought me – my car's in dock.' Felicity completed the introductions hastily, then returned to the subject that really concerned her. 'Peggy, what actually happened? Did he collapse?'

'No, nothing so dramatic. It was quite gradual. He started to complain of a crushing pain in his chest. Then it spread to his throat and left arm, by which time I was already ringing for an ambulance. Luckily, they had the equipment to start treating him right away and it couldn't have been more than half an hour after the first symptom before he was here.'

'Thank God you were on the spot,' Felicity said fervently. 'If he'd been alone... Peg, he's not going to die, is he?'

The older woman looked at her, and Felicity saw that there was fear as well as compassion in her eyes. Instinctively, without turning her head, she reached out for Jake and felt his hand clasp hers, warm and reassuring.

'They'll do the best they can for him, I know,' Peggy said gently, and Felicity nodded, the hot tears blurring her eyes.

'Why don't we all sit down,' Jake suggested, steering Felicity towards the long padded bench where Peggy had been waiting. 'We're in the way here, cluttering up the passage. The nurses can't get past.'

Felicity smiled in spite of her distress and sat down between the other two, feeling their warmth on either side of her like a fortress. She sat rigid, trembling slightly, her hands gripping each other tightly.

'Relax,' Jake murmured, and he covered her entwined fingers with his own. 'It's not going to do your father any good if you make yourself ill.'

'No.' But she turned and looked at him, her eyes terrified. 'But if he – if he doesn't get through this one, Jake, I don't know what I'm going to do. He's all I've got.'

Geoffrey would have reminded her that she had Grant Industrial Holdings and Stallymore Castle. He would have said something like 'You've got *me*, darling'. But Jake said neither of these things. He merely looked at her with eyes that understood, squeezed her hand in his and said quietly, 'I know. It's hard to lose your parents. And you lost your mother some time ago, didn't you?'

'When I was sixteen. She was killed in a road accident – run over by a bus. I'm over it now, but–'

'I don't think you ever really get over that kind of shock,' Jake observed soberly, and she glanced at him, surprised and grateful for his perception. 'And if you bottle it all up inside you, it's liable to break out at unexpected moments. You have to let these things out, Felicity, talk about them, over and over again if you feel the need. Otherwise it becomes impossible to show any emotion at all, for fear of touching that hidden spring.'

There was a movement beside them, and

Felicity sprang up to face the doctor who was emerging from the ward. He was accompanied by a nurse in sister's uniform. They stopped when they saw the three waiting in the corridor.

'Miss Grant?' the doctor said, holding out his hand. 'I'm Dr Fenning. I've just been examining your father.'

'How is he?' Her voice shook with tension.

'Not too bad at all, I'm glad to say. We've got him all fixed up and he's pretty comfortable. He's had an attack before, hasn't he? I won't pretend there's no risk of any further attacks. The next twenty-four hours or so are going to be fairly crucial. But if he goes on as he's doing at present, there's a good chance he'll pull through. D'you want to see him?'

'Oh, yes, please.'

'Well, you can, just for a moment. He mustn't be tired. Then I suggest you go home and have a good night's sleep before coming back in the morning. We've got a phone number for you, haven't we?'

'Yes,' Peggy said. 'I gave it with all his other details when we came in.'

'Good. Well, we'll be in touch with you at once should we think it necessary.' The doctor gave them a quick nod and brief, professional smile. 'Sister will see that you're looked after now. I know you'll excuse me – other patients to see.' He strode off down the corridor, his white coat flapping, and Felicity stared after him.

'But he didn't tell us *anything*. There are things I need to know. Sister–'

'There really isn't anything to tell at the moment,' the nurse said quietly. 'You know that your father suffers from angina. Normally, if he takes his tablets as soon as he feels the first signs, that's enough to ward off an attack. But more severe ones are likely to happen, unfortunately, though thanks to Mrs Whymark here, he was in hospital before too much damage could be done, at least as far as we can tell. As Dr Fenning said, it's really just a matter of keeping him quiet and monitoring his progress for the next few days. Anyway, come in now and have a quick word with him. He's conscious, but I want him to sleep as soon as possible, so I shan't let you stop long.'

'No, of course not.' Felicity moved towards the door, then paused and looked back at Jake. 'Will – will you come in with me?'

He demurred. 'Your father doesn't know me, Felicity. He can't want me at his bedside; it's you he wants to see.'

She wanted to say, *but I need you with me.* But her throat closed and the words wouldn't come. She felt Peggy's hand on her arm and knew that the sister was waiting. Slowly, she tiptoed into the room where her father lay waiting.

He looked smaller in the bed, his face as white as the pillow, with deep lines of pain etched in his cheeks. But when he saw her come in with Peggy, his tired eyes lit up and a small smile tugged feebly at his pale lips.

'Felicity... My dear...'

'Oh, Dad.' She sat down in the chair beside him, her hands on the white fingers lying on the smooth hospital bedspread. 'What have you been up to? Scaring us all like this!'

'Nothing to be scared about,' he murmured. 'Peggy had me in here ... almost before I knew I was ill ... I'll be all right. Playing golf again in a week or two, you'll see.'

'You'll do no such thing,' she told him severely. 'You'll look after yourself and do as you're told.'

'No fun in that,' he whispered. 'And I want some fun out of life now. There's not much time left. Never made the most of – opportunities–'

188

'Oh, Dad.' The tears spilled down her cheeks. 'You've nothing to regret, nothing to reproach yourself for. You've been a wonderful father to me.' She sought for something that might distract him. 'Guess who brought me down here, Dad. Jake Ashton. Remember I told you about him?'

'The painter?'

'That's right. He happened to be in the office when Peggy rang and insisted on bringing me. Wasn't that kind?'

'Kind,' he murmured and she knew he was falling asleep. 'Here now?'

'Yes. He's waiting for us outside.'

Her father whispered something, but the sound was too faint for her to catch. She bent lower.

'What is it, Dad? What do you want to say?'

'Want ... see the painter...'

'Tomorrow,' she said, her throat aching. 'I'll bring him to see you tomorrow. You go to sleep now. You'll feel better in the morning.'

'I'll have to ask you to go now,' the sister said quietly, and Felicity nodded and turned away, the tears running freely down her cheeks now, and followed Peggy outside.

Jake stepped forwards at once and took

her in his arms. Thankfully, she relaxed against his chest, feeling the steady heart-beat beneath her cheek and grateful for his silence. At last, feeling calmer, she looked up into his face.

'Thank you, Jake. I'm all right now.' She looked restlessly up and down the corridor. 'I don't think I'll go back to the house, Peggy. I'd rather stay here, within call – just in case.'

But Peggy shook her head. 'You'd be much better to come back and go to bed properly. You look tired out.'

'He'll sleep now for hours,' the sister confirmed. 'And we'll telephone you the moment anything happens, though I really don't expect it to now.'

'Let me take you back to the house,' Jake said, his arm still warm around her shoulders. 'It isn't far away, is it?'

'Only about ten minutes' drive,' Peggy told him, and his arm tightened on Felicity's shoulders, urging her gently towards the door.

'I promise I'll have you back here in less than eight, if you're needed,' he said, and Felicity looked up to see all the impishness gone from his expression, leaving it grave yet still with a warmth that touched her

190

heart. Suddenly, she saw him not as a joker, capering through life as if nothing really mattered, but as someone who had spent a considerable time in reflection, delving into the real meaning that lay beyond the superficiality that most people thought of as the 'real' world, as a man who could be relied upon in an emergency, a man who wouldn't immediately fill the air with unnecessary fuss and noise, but who would, quietly and efficiently, get things done.

'All right,' she said, capitulating. 'We'll go home. You – you will stay the night, won't you?'

'I won't go until you throw me out,' he promised, and she caught a glimpse of the old twinkle in his eyes and smiled in spite of her anxiety. 'On condition that if there's anything you want me to do, *anything,* you'll say so at once. Is that a deal?'

'It's a deal,' she said, and they touched hands briefly, their eyes meeting. And as they did so, Felicity experienced a tiny moment of recognition, of complete accord.

As if a deal had been made on some much deeper level.

Once back at the house, Peggy demonstrated her own quiet efficiency by making up a bed for Jake in the living room and then producing a supper of quiche and salad which was delicious enough to tempt even Felicity's appetite. It was followed by strawberries from the garden and ice-cream which Peggy had made herself.

'Poor Dad, missing this. He loves strawberries.' Felicity laid down her spoon and looked with tear-filled eyes at the crimson fruit. 'How can we eat like this, when he's lying there in that bed, perhaps even at this minute–'

'Now, stop that,' Peggy said firmly. 'It won't do your father any good for us to starve. And we might as well enjoy the food we've got. I can just imagine his expression when he comes out of hospital to find all his precious strawberries left to rot, just because we were too sensitive to eat them while he was ill. Where's the sense in that?'

'I know.' Felicity picked up her spoon again, though still without any great enthusiasm. 'Peggy, do you really believe he'll come out of hospital? It's his second attack, you know, and–'

'I know. And yes, I do believe he'll get over it, provided he doesn't have any more. He's in good hands, Felicity. They'll pull him through if anyone can.'

'And if they can't?'

'We'll just have to come to terms with it,' the older woman said quietly. 'Nobody's immortal, Felicity. But I don't think we're at that stage yet. There's still a lot of life left in your father. And he wants to recover. That counts for a lot.'

'He was talking about having fun,' Felicity said thoughtfully. 'Saying he'd never made the most of his opportunities. What did he mean by that?'

'Why don't you ask him yourself?' Peggy said. 'I'm sure he'll be only too glad to tell you, when he's feeling stronger. And I'm sure he will be, Felicity.' She rose briskly to her feet. 'Now I'm going to make you go to bed with a hot drink. You need some rest.'

'And so do you,' Jake said, getting up and collecting the dishes together with swift hands. 'You've been through a lot of stress today, Peggy, and you need bed and a hot drink too. I'll clear all this away and then I'll bring you both a mug of something soothing. No, I'll find everything. I'm a very useful man in a kitchen. I want you both in bed, sitting up and ready, in ten minutes, and no arguments, all right?'

Peggy gave him an amused glance, then looked at Felicity.

'He's a masterful man, this painter of yours, isn't he?' she remarked. 'Is he always as bossy as this?'

'No,' Felicity said, equally amused but only too thankful to fall in with Jake's commands. 'I've never seen him like it before.'

'It's one of the facets of my character you haven't encountered up till now,' Jake observed and added with a fierce expression, 'And if you don't go to bed at once, you'll encounter another one – so scoot!'

Felicity was in bed, as ordered, when Jake tapped on the door and came in with a tray. He set it down beside the bed and looked at her.

'Are you all right?'

Felicity nodded.

'Yes. I've got a phone extension here, so if the hospital phones it'll wake me at once. Not that I expect to sleep much.'

'Well, I hope you'll do your best. Staying awake worrying won't help your father any more than starving yourself. He won't want to see you tomorrow with dark circles under your eyes.'

'No.' Felicity struggled with the fear that

fluttered in her breast, and then looked up at Jake, her eyes wide and piteous. 'Jake, suppose I don't see him tomorrow? Suppose he – just goes?'

'They don't seem to think that's very likely.'

'But it could happen, couldn't it?' she persisted.

Jake looked at her for a moment. Then he sat down on the edge of her bed and took her hand.

'It could happen, yes,' he said steadily. 'But that's always on the cards, isn't it? None of us has guaranteed passage into old age. Something could happen to me, to you, to Peggy. Your father could outlive us all. You must know that,' he said gently, 'after losing your mother the way you did.'

Tears filled her eyes. 'I think perhaps that's why I'm so afraid,' she whispered. 'After Mum, there was only Dad left. My cousins – we never had much contact with them, apart from those summer holidays at Stallymore, and they're all scattered now. There was nobody else to share – things.'

'Such as your grief over your mother's death,' he said quietly.

'We never talked about it much. Dad couldn't bear to at first, and then later – I suppose we left it too late. Every time I tried, I felt myself getting upset, and it didn't seem fair on him, just when he was beginning to get over it. Except that he never really did, of course.'

'Which is not surprising, if he never talked about it. And you?'

'Me?'

'Did you ever talk about it with anyone else?'

'No, not really,' she said after a pause. 'There's never been anyone. At university, you see, most people had their parents intact, and since then–'

'Since then, you've been too busy building up Grant Holdings. And battening down your own feelings under an ever-thickening layer of self-control. No wonder your real self got buried, Felicity. The wonder is that she's still there at all. Though what shape she's in by now is anyone's guess.'

'I don't know what you mean.'

'No?' His dark eyes studied her. 'Just that you're playing with fire by refusing to face your emotions, Felicity. You see, it can have several effects. You may come to believe that the self you present to the world is your real self and be unable ever to relate to real emotion again. In other words, you'll be stunted. Or something might happen one day to release all that pent-up distress, like the breaking of a dam, with results that could be beneficial, but might equally be catastrophic, depending on the circumstances.'

Felicity stared at him. She wanted to refute his suggestions, but she was too exhausted. And she had an uncomfortable feeling that he might be striking very close to the truth. The self that she presented to the world – the cool, assertive business-woman who could control a Board made up mostly of men older than herself –was that the real Felicity? Once again, she had a brief mental picture of a leggy seven-year-old, exploring the woods. But I was only a child then, she argued, and a voice came back with the answer as swiftly and vividly as if someone had really spoken: but you *were* Felicity...

And if he were right, and the dam broke? She shivered suddenly, unable to imagine the disaster, the pain, that might follow.

'You seem to think you know all about me,' she said, her voice trembling a little as she looked down at the hand that covered hers. 'All this – it's just theory. You don't know any of it.'

'Perhaps not,' he agreed, 'but I do know what it is to lose my parents.'

'Oh!' Her head jerked up. 'I never thought ... you've never mentioned ... Jake, I'm sorry.'

'Did you imagine I'd sprung from nowhere?' he asked wryly. 'Well, why not? We don't go around enquiring into each other's family backgrounds. Well, I was older than you were when my mother died – in my early twenties. But it had been a pretty painful business. She had Alzheimer's disease – premature senility. It came on when she was only in her forties, and it took her fairly quickly, which is something to be thankful for, but we still had several years in which to see her go downhill. I was away then, so my father bore the brunt of it, but I went down as often as I could.'

'Jake, how terrible.'

'It wasn't a lot of fun,' he acknowledged. 'Nobody could be really sorry when it was all over. And yet there were all the memories from when she was well and full of life. Memories we shared – oh, of walks and picnics, the odd outing to Plymouth, holidays. Memories there was no one left to share with afterwards. And her own memories, too, the ones that went way back, to her own childhood, the days when she was a girl. All lost for ever.'

'Yes, I felt the same. But your father – he could share the memories with you.'

'Not for long. He couldn't live without her, it seemed. Never spoke a word about her after the funeral – but six months later, he was found dead in his car. Carbon monoxide poisoning.'

'Oh, no,' she whispered.

'I didn't come home for a long time after that,' he said quietly. 'Let the cottage. Stayed away, working as a commercial artist, mostly in advertising. But I could never quite bring myself to sell it. And when I did come back, to sort things out when my tenant left, I was glad I hadn't. I took one look at the cottage and saw suddenly what I really wanted. I'd had enough of the ratrace, the artificiality of all, and I knew I needed to get back to the grass roots of living. I stayed then and put the past where it belonged.' He looked at her, his eyes grave. 'It took me a long time to get my priorities right, Felicity, but I think I got there in the end, though others may not agree.'

He stood up and handed her the mug he had brought in. 'You'd better drink this before it gets completely cold.'

Felicity sipped it almost without noticing. Her mind was still shaken by the story of heartbreak and tragedy that Jake had just told her. She thought of her own parents – her mother, killed so early, so unnecessarily. But at least she hadn't had to go through a terrible, debilitating illness. And her father, living contentedly with Peggy. Perhaps he talked to his housekeeper and friend about the wife he had lost eleven years ago. Perhaps he had at last come to terms with his grief.

'Sleep well,' Jake said, and bent to kiss her, very gently. 'You know where I am if you need anything.'

She looked up at him. She wanted to ask him to stay, to give her warmth and comfort through the night. But even as their eyes met, she saw him shake his head, very slightly, and knew that his way was best. He had given her food for thought; now she needed sleep, to let his words sink into her brain, to absorb what he had told her. And to be ready to go to her father in the morning.

'Mr Grant's a lot better this morning,' the sister on duty told them as they arrived at the hospital soon after breakfast. 'He's awake and looking forward to seeing you. You can go straight in.'

'That means you too,' Felicity said to Jake. 'He asked to see you today.'

She led the way into the side ward, feeling a good deal more optimistic this morning. An early telephone call to the hospital had brought the news that her father had had a good night and would be able to see visitors as soon as they liked to arrive. He was still weak from the shock of the attack, but provided they kept the visit brief and restricted to no more than two people, it should do him nothing but good.

Jake had at first demurred, but Peggy told him briskly that she had plenty to do at home and would go in later during the morning. She would be spending most of her time at the hospital anyway, once Felicity had gone home, and it was a load off her mind to know that Felicity had Jake to support her.

To Felicity's relief, her father did indeed look better. There was a little colour in the cheeks that had been so waxen, and his faded eyes had brightened. As they entered, he tried to pull himself up in the bed, but she put her hand on his shoulder and pressed him gently back against the pillow.

'Dad, you are looking better. The holiday obviously suits you!'

'It's the nurses,' he said. 'I don't get all these pretty girls to wait on me at home. I'm thinking of taking one with me.' His eyes went past Felicity to Jake, standing just inside the door. 'So you're Jake Ashton. My daughter's told me about you.'

'It's all lies,' Jake said, coming forward. 'I'm glad to meet you, Mr Grant, though sorry it has to be in these circumstances.'

'It's just a cry for attention, really,' the older man said, his voice still weak. 'I have to do these things to get my daughter to visit me. It's hard, being old and neglected.' He smiled faintly at Felicity's protest. 'How is the picture coming along?'

'Pretty well. I'm getting everyone sorted out now. I hope to start the canvas itself next week – been working on sketches up to now.'

'It's a big job,' John Grant said, and closed his eyes as though he felt suddenly exhausted.

Felicity stepped forward with an anxious glance. 'Are you all right, Dad? Is there anything you need? The nurse–?'

'No, I'm all right. Just a little tired. Sit beside me for a while, will you?'

'Of course.' Felicity glanced at Jake, who

stepped aside so that she could move round the narrow space into the chair.

'I'll wait outside,' he murmured, and she nodded, sitting down beside her father and taking his thin hand. Her eyes blurred as she looked at the veins, the wrinkles, the brown spots. It was the hand of an old man.

Yet her father was only in his late sixties. What had happened to him, to age him so soon, when others lived on filled with vitality into their eighties and beyond?

'Jake Ashton,' he murmured and she turned her eyes back to his face. 'He seems ... a good man.'

Felicity nodded. 'He is. At first, I thought he was a bit of a fool – an eccentric artist, living in a world of his own. But as I've gradually got to know him, I've begun to see that there's a lot more to him than that. He's been a tower of strength these past two days.'

'He's that sort.' John Grant spoke in short phrases, resting between each one. 'Got his own ideas ... about things ... I should think.'

'He certainly has,' Felicity agreed, a smile in her voice. 'Poor Geoffrey is completely bemused by him.'

'Not thinking of marrying ... Geoffrey ... are you?'

Felicity looked at him, startled. 'No, I'm not.' She spoke with a decision that surprised herself. 'Whatever made you ask that?'

'Thought you two ... were getting friendly. Not the man for you, Felicity. . .' There was a long pause. 'Need someone more ... in tune with real life...' He was clearly tiring now and making an effort to go on talking. 'Don't waste your life ... thinking about business ... Have some fun. Laughing's important, Felicity ... remember that ...' His eyes opened suddenly and he looked at her with a trace of his old vigour, as if trying to impart some great truth. 'Don't ever forget...'

'I won't.' She held his hand close, her heart aching with distress. 'Dad, please don't talk any more. You need to rest. Go to sleep now.'

He smiled faintly and closed his eyes as if content now that he had said what he wanted to. In a moment, he was breathing gently and she released her hand from his and tiptoed to the door.

Jake was sitting outside. He jumped to his feet as she came out of the ward.

'Is anything...?'

'It's all right. He's asleep. Jake, I'm going

204

to stay here with him as long as they'll let me. If he wakes, he'll see me there. Peggy's coming in later. You might as well go back.'

Jake shook his head. 'I'll stay too. I've nothing else to do,' he said when she began to protest. 'I'm just as well here as anywhere, and I may be able to be useful. If you need anything, just poke your head out, all right? I'll be around.'

Felicity smiled gratefully at him and went back to her father. She sat down beside him again and took his hand, watching the screen beside him that showed the pattern of his heartbeat. And as she sat there throughout the long, quiet morning, she thought over everything that had happened, everything that had been said during the last twelve hours.

She thought of Jake, telling her she must face up to her emotions, set the real Felicity free. She remembered the tragic story of his own parents. She thought of her father, whispering that Geoffrey wasn't the man for her. Telling her to remember that laughter was important.

And as she sat there, trying to transmit her own strength through the thin, weak hand she held, she thought of the gnawing pain of the weeks, the months after her mother had died, the pain that could not be released and had been driven deeper, deeper within her until it was buried almost too deeply to find.

The tears came into Felicity's eyes and overflowed. She began at last to weep for her mother.

Eight

'I must say,' Geoffrey said, 'I was somewhat surprised to hear that you'd gone to Bournemouth with Ashton. It seemed a little odd, to say the least.'

'I told you before, Jake happened to be with me when the phone call came through. And with my car in dock – everything happened so fast, Geoff. I was just thankful to accept his offer.' Felicity rubbed a hand across her eyes. She felt more exhausted now, a week after her hurried flight to Bournemouth, than she had while she had been there, spending every spare moment at the hospital, watching her father with an anxiety that wouldn't let her believe he was truly out of the wood until the heart specialist had assured her that he was likely to make a full recovery.

'You could have rung me, all the same. I'd have come at once. Surely you knew that.'

Felicity looked at him and smiled tiredly. 'Yes, Geoff, I know. But I couldn't think of anything just then other than getting to Dad as quickly as possible. And since Jake–'

'Happened to be with you when the call came. I know.' Geoffrey pursed his lips. 'But wasn't this call quite late? After everyone had gone home? Just what–'

'Was Jake doing in the office then?' Felicity finished for him. 'He'd just come in to talk, I suppose. He hadn't been in for a couple of days. Not since–' She blushed as she remembered the encounter between the three of them in her bathroom. 'Well, anyway, he just looked in. He was only here for a moment before Peggy rang. Geoffrey, please, I'd rather not argue about this. The important thing was to get to Dad – it hardly mattered who took me.'

'No, I suppose not.' Geoffrey made a visible effort and then smiled at her. 'And your father's really on the mend?'

'They're very happy with him. They expect to send him home in a day or two.'

'Well, that's wonderful. We must arrange a

welcome-home party for him.'

'Geoff, he's coming home from hospital. He's had a heart attack. I don't think–'

'No. Perhaps you're right. Anyway, I'm glad everything's all right again. Now, if you'd like to go through what we've been doing while you were away.' He opened the top file of the stack he had brought in with him and began to talk. Felicity listened, putting a question now and then, but the main part of her mind was elsewhere.

She had already intended to provide a small welcoming party for her father. Nothing elaborate, just a quiet gathering composed of herself, Peggy – and Jake. Not Geoffrey.

During the few days she and Jake had spent in Bournemouth, the artist had visited her father several times and the two of them had become friends immediately. Twice, Felicity had left them alone together while she went out to do a little shopping for her father, and each time she'd come back to find them chortling over some joke which they refused to explain. Jake had taken his sketch pad in and amused John Grant by producing lightning sketches of both himself and the staff who nursed him. Sketches which somehow found their way on to the walls of the small room where he was being treated. Even Dr Fenning had been unable to repress a smile at the sight, and Night Sister had asked if she could keep her sketch when Mr Grant went home.

Once they had been freed from their acute anxiety about her father, Felicity and Jake had treated the short time in Bournemouth as a holiday, going for long walks along the clifftops when Peggy was with John, or making excursions into the New Forest. Relaxed, feeling her inhibitions slip away under Jake's influence, Felicity had found herself talking more freely than ever before. And she had seen more, too. The changing colours of the sea and sky, taken so often for granted, the cool green of the ancient trees of the Forest, the peace of a clearing or tiny, deserted cove, all sharply experienced, as if mists had cleared from her eyes to show her the world she had walked through for so long without really noticing.

Now she was back at Stallymore Castle. And, listening to Geoffrey's serious voice, watching his pallid face, she began to wonder just what it was all about.

'Oh, let's leave it for a while,' she broke in at last as he reached out for yet another file. 'We've been at it now for almost two hours.

209

It's a lovely morning outside, Geoff. Let's take our coffee outside and have it in the gardens. Jackie can bring hers too – that girl works too hard.'

Geoffrey dropped the file and stared at her, astonishment rounding his light blue eyes.

'Take our coffee outside? But we've got a lot to get through, Felicity. I was going to suggest a working lunch, just a few sandwiches here at your desk.'

'Thanks, but no thanks.' Felicity pressed the switch on the intercom. 'Jackie, Mr Hall and I are having our coffee in the garden and we'd like you to join us. In about five or ten minutes, all right?' She smiled at Geoffrey. 'It'll do you good to get some fresh air. You're looking quite pale for the time of year.'

'Whereas you look as tanned as if you'd just come back from holiday,' he retorted. 'Look, Felicity, I think it's time you and I had a serious talk. There hasn't been a chance since that unfortunate affair the other week.'

'When you found me and Jake in my bathroom, you mean,' Felicity said helpfully.

Geoffrey reddened. 'I didn't want to refer to it so specifically, but since you evidently feel no embarrassment about it, yes. Anyway, if you recall, I made a proposition – a proposal–'

'Call it a proposition,' Felicity said steadily. 'It really had much more to do with business than anything else, don't you agree?'

'Felicity, you're not making this easy for me. Very well, I made a certain proposition and suggested you should think it over. Well, I imagine by now you've had time, so I'd be grateful if you'd tell me if you've come to any decision.'

Felicity gazed at him. The sheer effrontery of the man left her almost speechless. Did he really believe that there was even a remote possibility of her accepting him and his so-called proposal? Did he really think she looked or behaved like a woman who was about to agree to a proposal of marriage?

'Geoffrey, I told you my decision then,' she said. 'And as I recall, you didn't so much propose to me as threaten me. Or had you forgotten that?'

Geoffrey looked irritated. 'That was just a manner of speaking, Felicity. You'd annoyed me, I admit. I didn't expect you to take it seriously.'

'You mean you won't tell the Board you found me playing bullfights in the bathroom with Jake Ashton? I'm truly grateful, Geoffrey. But that doesn't alter the fact that you behaved like a bully that day, and even if I had been considering marriage to you, I would have abandoned the idea immediately. I'm sorry to be so blunt, Geoff, but I think it's necessary. I don't want you assuming any proprietorial rights over me. And I think it's best if from now on we meet only in the office or on official business. I shall certainly do my best to keep such meetings on a friendly level, and I hope you will too. Now, I'm going to have coffee out in the garden, looking at the beautiful roses, and I'd like you to come too. If you don't want to, we'll continue our meeting later. After lunch.'

Geoffrey got to his feet. His face was a dark, angry red and Felicity looked at him and felt a sudden stab of unease. It was quite clear that she'd made an enemy of Geoffrey, and that was a bad move. But there was nothing to be done about it now. She made her smile as friendly as possible and held out a hand, but Geoffrey ignored it. He picked up his files.

'I'll be in my own office if you need me,'

he said stiffly. 'Having coffee at my desk.' He stalked towards the door, then paused and looked back.

'I hope you're not going to regret this attitude of yours, Felicity,' he told her. 'You've done well so far, no one denies that. But you've had a good team behind you. Lose their confidence, and you could lose a whole lot more. Think about it.' And then he opened the door and was gone.

And what was that? Felicity wondered as she went down the stairs to join Jackie, who had already taken the coffee tray down to a seat on the lawn. Another veiled threat?

The lane to Jake's cottage was, as Jackie had warned her, rough and unmade. Felicity nosed her car slowly between high banks thick with the creamy lace of wild parsley, negotiating deep ruts and jutting rocks with care. No wonder not many people ventured up here!

She was aware this evening was another important stage in her relationship with Jake. Jackie had told her that he seldom entertained visitors, and Felicity did not underestimate the importance of his apparently casual invitation to supper. She felt a tingling curiosity to see just what Jake's

213

home was like. She was aware that it would tell her more about the man himself, and understood why he had wanted to see her own flat.

The cottage stood at the end of the track, sheltered from the open moor by a small wood that curved around it on three sides. Facing south, it looked soaked in sun, and as Felicity parked her car and got out she saw that a wooden seat at one end of the cottage was bathed in evening light.

She stood for a moment, her hand on the gate, gazing at the scene before her.

It was larger than she had expected, probably once a farmhouse, long and low with a thickly-thatched roof with eaves like shaggy eyebrows. The garden wandered all around it, a riot of tall meadowgrass filled with wild flowers, the purple spires of foxglove melting into the soft pink of rosebay willowherb, the glory of honeysuckle tangling with the pink and white of dog roses in the hedgerow. A few old fruit trees, their trunks and branches gnarled with age, gave shade in one corner and a cloud of butterflies rose from a huge buddleia bush in another.

'So there you are.' Jake strolled round the corner of the house, casual in a loose shirt and old jeans. 'Thought I heard a car. Ten points for perseverance – some fainthearts leave their precious vehicles at the bottom of the lane.' He grinned, reached out a long arm and drew her to him for a firm, brief kiss. 'Nice to see you again,' he said, smiling down at her.

'Nice to see you, too.' She felt suddenly breathless and added quickly, 'Jake, this is lovely. So peaceful and quiet.'

'Mm,' he said, 'I like it. It suits me to be away from the maddening crowd. And I'm quite civilised too – don't even have to draw water from the well, these days. Though I haven't made it to the chlorinated pleasures of mains water yet.'

'You have your own supply?'

'And my own disposal system.' He grinned at her expression. 'Don't worry, you can't tell. It works just like the real thing. No earth privies.'

'Well, I'm glad to hear that!' They moved slowly along one of the paths mown through the long grass. 'And when are you going to start on the garden?' she enquired innocently.

Jake gave a shout of laughter. 'Felicity, you're wonderful! You really mean that, don't you? You really think I should be cutting all this long grass to within an inch of its life, mowing down all these wild flowers, shaving the hedges bare.' He stopped and looked at her more closely. 'No, you don't. You're just winding me up. You know very well this is the way I like my garden.'

Felicity smiled. 'It's not often anyone catches you out, Jake. That'll have to go down in history. Yes, I had realised the garden was like this from choice. But why?'

'Because this is how God wants it,' he said, 'with all the natural inhabitants: the grasses, the wild flowers, the shrubs and hedges. Look at those butterflies, Felicity – have you ever seen such a show? Red Admirals, tortoiseshells, peacocks, painted ladies – half the butterflies you see in my garden have become rarities in our own lifetimes. Don't you think that's a tragedy?'

'Yes, I do,' she said slowly, watching the brilliant kaleidoscope of colour as the butterflies fed greedily on the nectar of the flowers. 'But why is it? What happened to them?'

'We happened to them,' he said soberly. 'Man, with all his marvellous sprays and insecticides and noisy machinery and pollution. We're killing this planet, Felicity.

The few wildernesses we've got left are vital, not just to save a few butterflies, but to us all. Well, maybe we can't all do much about the big areas – that's up to big business and governments – but we can all do something towards our own little patch.' He paused for a moment. 'Someone I respected very much once said to me that if everyone tended the bit outside his own front door, the whole world would be safe.'

'But you don't tend this,' she said, looking at the grass.

'I look after it, though,' he said. 'I save it from the kind of over-tending so many people take a pride in doing. I keep it for the wild things: the insects, the birds and animals that are being driven out of so many places. There are birds nesting all round here. Hedgehogs snuffling round the hedges. Badgers in the woods. And I do do a certain amount of husbandry – the grass benefits from being cut a couple of times during the year, and a neighbour likes the hay for her goat. In fact, it's recycled over and over again, since she lets me have the end product, as it were, for manure!'

He led her round the end of the cottage to the back door. 'Come inside. I'm a true countryman, you see – the front door's used only for weddings and funerals. I'm not even sure where it is any more, from the inside.'

Felicity followed him into the dim kitchen. It was larger than she had expected, a true farmhouse kitchen fitted out with cupboards of light oak, a solid-fuel cooker and modern refrigerator. A normal electric cooker and hob were neatly fitted into the worktop and the middle of the room was taken up by a large pine table, soft with the golden sheen of age and much polishing.

'This is lovely!' she exclaimed. 'Did you have it done when you moved back here?'

'Did it myself,' Jake said, pinning a piece of sketch paper to one of the beams that crossed the low ceiling. Felicity moved across and found that it was a pencil sketch of two birds on a nest filled with the wide-open beaks of fledglings. She looked at it curiously, and noticed that there were similar sketches along the length of the beam.

'I didn't know you were so interested in wildlife,' she observed.

'Didn't you? Come through and have a drink.' He led the way through a low doorway, ducking automatically to avoid bumping his head. 'This is the main room. It runs along the length of the front of the

218

house. Used to be two rooms, with a passage in between. As you see, there's a front door somewhere!'

'If you say so,' Felicity smiled. She looked round with interest. The room was long and light, with windows on both sides of the doorway which had been effectively blocked by an easel. Several sofas and armchairs of no particular design, though each one looked enticingly comfortable, were scattered about the room. At some time they had all been given loose covers which had, like the curtains at the windows, faded to a blur of soft colour, like a garden seen in twilight. There was a fireplace piled with wood, and two of the walls were lined with shelves. Jake evidently had a wide-ranging taste in reading, thought Felicity, picking out titles by Dick Francis, Iris Murdoch and Proust. The rest of the walls were covered in paintings and sketches, and in one corner there was a rack hung with a rainbow of coloured waistcoats.

Felicity thought of her own stark living room, designed to impress clients and colleagues. Jake clearly had no interest in making an impression. This was his home and he lived in it in his own way – and why not?

'Well?' he said, and the familiar note of amusement was there in his voice. 'Aren't you going to ask me when I'm going to tidy up?'

Felicity laughed. 'No, I'm not! Though I suppose if the police were called they might say there was evidence of a struggle. Jake, did you do these bird paintings on the wall? And these beautiful ones of an otter and the young badgers?'

'Guilty.' He poured the drinks and came over to stand beside her. 'I watched those badgers every night for three weeks,' he said softly. 'They've got a sett up in the woods. I used to go up there before dark, then wait for them to come out. You have to stay absolutely still – a flicker of movement or a whiff of human scent and they're back inside before you can say *Wind in the Willows.*'

'But how could you see them, if they don't come out until dark?'

'Moonlight.'

'For three weeks?' she asked sceptically, and he grinned.

'Trust my Felicity to spot the flaw! No, on really dark nights I used red light. A flashlight with a red bulb, or with red cellophane over the glass. Badgers don't see red light. I got quite attached to those little chaps,' he said reflectively, looking at the painting which showed the cubs tumbling over the recumbent body of their mother. 'Even gave them names.'

Felicity gave him an uncertain glance. 'You sound rather sad. Have they all gone?'

'Sad? I'm not sure that's the word.' He turned away. 'Thinking of those youngsters brings me the nearest I've ever got to wanting to commit murder. You see, I wasn't the only one who knew about that sett. And one night, when I went up there to see how things were, I found someone else had been there first. The sett was torn open and the nesting material the parents used to bring out to air every night was scattered. Maybe some of them survived; they might even come back someday. I keep hoping.'

Felicity stared at him, horrified. 'But what? – who?'

'Badger-baiters,' he said succinctly. 'They go with dogs. Badgers will fight to the death, you know. Apparently, they see it as a sport.'

'But – it must be against the law.'

'Oh, it is – if they're caught. What haunts me is that I only missed going to see the sett

221

on one night, and that had to be the night they struck. If I'd been there...'

Felicity looked again at the picture. The tumbling cubs, so full of life, seemed almost to leap out at her. She felt an ache in her throat.

'Where did you see the otter?'

'Oh, down by the river. I've never told anyone exactly where. Otters are becoming so rare in this country, they're approaching extinction. I don't want to risk my badger friends finding out about them – you see, I've never been able to rid myself of the notion that I might have given them away somehow. Everyone knew I was drawing badgers – I did quite a few pictures of them and showed them locally. It wouldn't take much to deduce where they were, especially if anyone bothered to keep an eye on my movements.'

'Is that why you don't show your work in the gallery?' Felicity asked, remembering the night when she and Geoffrey had met him in Exeter.

'Partly. And because it's too much hassle, having to decide which pictures to take, getting them all ready, transporting them there. Plus the humiliation of bringing most of them back unsold,' he added with a grin.

Felicity laughed. 'I'm sure that doesn't happen much.'

'Oh, you'd be surprised. Not everyone likes tasteful representations of the English country scene. Now, if I were painting dock scenes, with tower cranes tangling their long necks against the skyline like an everlasting spider's web...'

'I wouldn't give it houseroom,' Felicity said firmly. 'I think these are much nicer.'

Jake gave her a long look, and she remembered that on her own walls she had a painting not so very different from the one he had just described. She blushed deeply. 'You know, I don't really like that picture I've got,' she said honestly. 'In fact, I don't like any of them. I'm going to change the whole room – redecorate, refurnish, everything.'

'Make it more like your bedroom?' he asked, eyes dancing.

'Make it more like me,' she said, and took a step towards him.

They stood quite still for a moment, almost close enough to touch each other. The look that passed between them was as intimate and as eloquent as a kiss. Felicity felt suddenly short of breath and her heart kicked violently against her ribs. She touched her lips with the tip of her tongue.

Jake moved away. 'So the real Felicity is still emerging, like a butterfly from its chrysalis,' he said lightly. 'Well, I hope the transformation is making you hungry. I've got a chicken casserole in the oven that it would be a crime not to eat now, at the moment of peak perfection.'

'Then we'd better eat it.' Felicity, hardly knowing whether to feel disappointed or relieved, followed him back to the kitchen. 'I don't want to be arrested.'

'Oh, I don't know,' he murmured. 'I could detain you on suspicion.' He opened a drawer and pulled out some table mats, handing her the cutlery to set beside them. 'Glasses in that cupboard,' he told her, taking a bottle of wine out of the fridge. A bowl of salad was set in the middle of the table, and then Jake took warm plates from the lower oven. Finally out came the casserole and a bowl of new potatoes, smelling of fresh mint. 'There. That's it, I think.'

'You know,' Felicity said a few minutes later, swallowing her first mouthful, 'you can cook. This is absolutely delicious.'

'Don't be too sure,' he warned. 'For all you know, this is the only thing I can do. Or maybe I have a "woman" to come and cook for me. You should never go by appearances, Felicity.'

'No, I've learned that,' she murmured, thinking of the first time she had seen Jake himself, and he gave her a bright glance, as if reading her mind. Hastily, she changed the direction of her thinking and fell into what had become a regular game of hers lately – comparing him with Geoffrey. Perhaps it was because they were the only two men she had known well since her university days, but the contrast between them never failed to fascinate her.

What, for instance, would Geoffrey have given her if he had invited her to supper in his 'executive cottage'? Not that he was ever likely to have done so. Geoffrey much preferred eating out, his entertaining made easy for him by an unseen army of cooks and bottlewashers. Probably he would have resorted to frozen foods – of the classiest kind, naturally – or, as Jake had suggested, persuaded his 'daily' to cook a meal and leave it for him to serve.

After the meal, they washed up together – another thing that could never have happened in Geoffrey's tiny, immaculate kitchen – and took their coffee out to the garden to watch the dusk gather slowly in its corners. The butterflies had disappeared now and only a few birds sang as they settled down for the night. The sun had become no more than a soft apricot glow in the west, and the sky was deepening to a velvety indigo. Felicity breathed in the scent of stocks and then jumped slightly as she heard a rustling close by.

'It's all right,' Jake murmured, his hand on her bare arm. 'It's only Hodge.'

'Hodge?'

He nodded his head slightly, indicating in which direction she should look, and Felicity glanced down to see the shuffling form of a hedgehog leave the shadow of the hedge and make its way purposefully along one of Jake's mown paths. Intent on his own business, he took no notice of the two watchers, but snuffled busily through the grass, pausing now and then to examine something, then going on as hurriedly as if he had an appointment he dared not miss.

'There's a family of them somewhere about,' Jake remarked. 'I haven't found them. I don't go looking for nests and such, it never seems fair to disturb them by poking about just out of curiosity. But I daresay Mrs Hodge will bring them all out one evening to entertain me.'

'And you'll be here to see them,' Felicity said. 'I envy you your life, Jake. No sudden panics, no phone calls demanding that you go up to London or even abroad to settle some business contract, no long days spent with solicitors and accountants.'

'Just the odd badger-baiter or bird-nester,' he agreed, and she was silenced. After a moment, he went on, 'We do all have a choice in how we live our lives, Felicity.'

'I know, but—'

'And if we make a mistake the first time around, we can often change direction.'

'It's not always that easy.'

'Are you regretting your way of life?' he asked. 'Seeing big business turn sour on you?'

'No! It suits me – I'm a career woman. It's all I've ever wanted to do. You can ask my father if that's true. I always wanted to go into the business with him.'

'But you've done more than that,' he pointed out. 'The business your father ran was a small local printing works. He printed things like programmes and dance tickets for local clubs, letter-headings, that sort of thing. He was never in business as you are, with fingers in all those other pies.'

'But that's the way it works now. You expand, or you go under.'

'And is that the only way?'

'It's the only way for me,' she said stubbornly. 'I've built up what I have and I'm proud of it. And I couldn't stop now if I wanted to – the Board wouldn't let me.'

'Ah, yes,' he said. 'The Board.' He was silent for a moment, and then he said, 'Don't you ever see that Board as a kind of Frankenstein, Felicity, a monster you've created and which now rules you?'

'No, I don't!' She jumped to her feet, the peace of the evening ruined by his probing. 'Jake, why are you doing this? I was happy enough until you came into my life. Now – now, I don't know where I am. I don't even know who I am!'

'But you're finding out,' he said quietly. 'For the first time in years, you're beginning to ask questions.'

Felicity turned and stared down at him. It was too dark now to see his face clearly. She lifted both hands to her face and swayed a little.

'Jake,' she whispered, 'what's happening? What are you doing to me?'

Jake stood up and took her in his arms. She rested against him, conscious of his warmth and strength, closing her eyes against the rest of the world.

'You know what I'm doing to you, Felicity,' he said quietly, and lifted her face to his.

She received his kiss with a kind of desperation, returning it as if searching for something she had sought for years. Her tongue met his, her lips clung to his, and she strained her body against him, feeling that even the thin clothes they both wore were too heavy a barrier between them. If only she were naked, as she'd been the first time he had kissed her! With a groan that tore its way up from her breast, she arched herself towards him and let her head fall back so that he could bend his head to her throat.

'Love me, Jake,' she whispered. 'Love me. Please'

He ran a trembling hand over her taut breasts, and then slipped his fingers beneath her shoulders to bring her upright again. Her head fell against his shoulder.

'No, Felicity,' he said quietly. 'Not tonight. It still isn't time.'

'But why not? Don't you want me?' She dragged his head down to hers, covered his face with frantic kisses, and felt him shake in her arms.

'Want you? My God, I want you! But it would be too easy...' With what seemed to be a supreme physical effort, he held her away from him. 'Felicity, you've got a long way to go yet. I could make love to you now, and we'd both enjoy it. But I want our first lovemaking to mean more than that. I want it to mean a commitment, an expression of real understanding of each other. Do you know what I mean?'

'I just want to love you,' she whispered, and saw the glimmer of his teeth as he smiled.

'When you know what I mean,' he said, 'you'll be ready. And now, I think you should go home.'

'I don't want—'

'Please,' he said, and she knew that she would do as he asked.

As she drove home, Felicity felt the turmoil within her churn like the troubled waters of a whirlpool. The tranquillity of the night seemed to be no more than a mockery of the emotions that beat wildly within her. Yet she felt none of the hurt pride that she might have expected, after having offered herself to a man and been refused. And perhaps, she thought, that was a sign that she was groping at least some way towards the understanding that Jake demanded.

Yet just what was that understanding? What kind of commitment did he want? Was it yet another replay of the old tune – a man who wanted her to give up her career in favour of his?

Jake hadn't expressed it like that – but what other explanation could there be?

She drove the car into the garage that had been converted from the old stable and walked across to the door that led into her garden. As she unlocked the french windows, she heard the telephone ringing.

Dad! He'd had another attack.

Felicity stumbled across the room and grabbed the telephone. She put it to her ear.

'Yes? Hullo? Who is it? Peggy, is that you?'

A male voice, sounding a little puzzled, said, 'Is that Felicity Grant?'

'Yes – who is it? What's wrong?'

'I'm not quite sure,' the voice said. 'But I think we ought to have a meeting straight away. There's something odd going on, and you ought to know about it as soon as possible.'

'Something odd?' Felicity stared at the instrument as if it could be persuaded to tell her more. 'What are you talking about? Who are you?'

'Oh, sorry,' the voice said. 'I thought you'd recognise me. It's Michael Butterford here. I need to see you – to talk about the Haverford contract.'

Nine

'Sir Michael.' Felicity went forward at once as he stepped out of his Daimler. 'It's good of you to come so early. We'll go into my flat and talk there, where we can be undisturbed. I've left a note on my secretary's desk to tell her I may be in late.'

The big man followed her across the gravel to her garden door and into the living room, barely appearing to notice his surroundings. He sat down in one of the leather armchairs and opened his briefcase.

Felicity poured a cup of the coffee which she had already prepared, and waited nervously.

'You said you wanted to talk about the Haverford contract,' she said after a moment. 'Has something gone wrong?'

'I don't know.' He frowned. 'Felicity, I may be acting unconventionally in coming to you like this. You're expanding so fast, we could easily become rivals. But I don't like skullduggery, and especially I don't like moles. I've always believed in fair dealing, though that seems to be going out of fashion now.'

Felicity stared at him. The side of big business that he referred to – the wheeling and dealing, the underhandedness of some operations that depended for success on betrayal and a devious interpretation of company law, had always been repugnant to her, and so far she believed that she had managed to steer Grant Holdings clear of any such taint. But if she had heard Sir Michael correctly–

'Are you saying there's something questionable about the Haverford contract?' she asked.

'There's something very odd about it.' He laid the papers down on the low table. 'Look at these figures, Felicity. And these.'

'Those aren't the figures we produced,' she said after a moment.

'No. Precisely. And there's more.' In a few words, he outlined to her the extent of his worries, while Felicity gazed at him in dawning horror. Evidence of insider dealing ... whispers on the Stock Exchange ... talk of mergers and takeovers... She shook her head unbelievingly.

'But this could ruin Grant Holdings,' she said at last. 'And how is it I've never heard anything of this? I don't understand.'

'You've been a little unreachable during the past week or two,' Sir Michael pointed out, and she remembered the week spent at her father's bedside, her impatient order to the office that the members of the Board should deal with whatever came up. 'And there's been nothing really concrete, not until these figures came into my hands last night.'

'But what does it mean? You talked about a mole.'

'I did.' He looked grim. 'It's my belief that there's someone at Stallymore who has his own interests at heart rather more than the company's. Who that is, you ought to know better than I.'

Felicity gazed at him. Her mind wanted to refute his allegation, but she knew she must be realistic. Someone, someone who had her confidence and knew a good deal about the operation of the Haverford contract as well as several other Grant projects, had clearly begun to work on his own account. But who could it be?

A thin, dark face came into her mind. Eyes

like prunes, discoloured teeth, a barely concealed dislike of being ruled by a woman.

'Suppose I could think of someone,' she said hesitantly. 'What ought I to do about it?'

Sir Michael leaned forward. 'It's not too late to put a stop to this, provided you act quickly. I've been watching the performance of your shares. Nothing to worry about yet, but let these whispers gather strength and there could be a run on them. Once get a panic on, and you've got problems. And that's when whoever this man's working for will step in and buy you out. It's happened before, Felicity. Before you know what's hit you, Grant Holdings will be split up and vanish.'

'Asset stripping,' Felicity said, and he nodded.

'Exactly that.'

She felt a cold fear grip her. Was this really happening? And just at the moment when life had begun to mean something different, something more to her? For a moment, she was tempted to tell Sir Michael that she'd had enough, that this kind of angst wasn't what she'd gone into business for, she didn't need it. But then her mind began to work again, overriding her emotions. Of course she couldn't simply abandon Grant Holdings to its fate! People depended on her keeping a steady hand on the wheel. The shareholders, the employees, the members of the Board.

One of whom was a traitor.

With a sick feeling in her stomach, she asked, 'What should I do?'

'The first thing,' Sir Michael said, 'is to talk to your Board. Call a meeting at once and bring the whole thing out into the open. That should flush him out. There's nothing moles hate more than daylight.'

'Yes.' She knew he was right, but she wasn't looking forward to it. Desperately, she wished that her father were well and strong, so that she could ask his advice. But that was impossible. 'Sir Michael, would you attend the Board meeting?'

He looked regretful. 'I'd be only too pleased. But I've got to go to Germany for a few days on business – something that can't be put off, I'm afraid.' He glanced at his watch. 'In fact, I'll have to be away soon, I've got to get to Exeter for the morning shuttle to Heathrow.' He looked at her and his kindly face softened. 'Don't worry, Felicity. You'll cope. You're a strong woman and you've got a good head. I'm only sorry you're not on *my* Board.'

He stood up and Felicity rose to see him out. Thoughtfully, she followed him out to the drive where a row of cars indicated the office staff and other Board members had begun to arrive. She wondered what they had made of seeing Sir Michael's Daimler parked there so early.

One man, at least, might have had a good idea as to why he might have come.

Nigel Earnshaw was the last to arrive at the hastily-convened Board meeting. Felicity's cousin Andrew, now back in Spain, was absent but it seemed hardly likely that he should be implicated in the affair. The rest of the members watched her as she took her seat, with varying degrees of curiosity, interest and wariness.

'Well?' Geoffrey demanded as soon as she was seated. 'What's all this about, Felicity? Your message said it was urgent.' His tone implied that, since he didn't know the reason himself, this was likely to have been an exaggeration.

'And so it is.' Felicity paused and allowed her eyes to move slowly over the faces around the table. 'Ladies and gentlemen, I'm afraid we have something rather serious to discuss this morning. I've had a visit from Sir Michael Butterford.' She caught a quick movement, instantly suppressed, from somewhere on her right. 'He's given me some rather disturbing news.' She paused again.

'Well, come on then, let's have it,' Geoffrey said impatiently. 'You did call me away from some rather important work of my own, you know.'

Felicity glanced at him and then at Nigel Earnshaw, who was watching her with narrow-eyed attention. She took a deep breath.

'According to Sir Michael,' she said, 'we have a mole among us. Someone has been leaking our plans, especially over the Haverford contract. As you know, it's the biggest, most ambitious project we've tackled yet, and if anything goes wrong the whole company could go to the wall.' She had all their attention now. The room was still, quiet, everyone watching her. 'Our whole future, the future of the company, of hundreds of employees and thousands of shareholders is at stake here,' she said quietly. 'We must find out the source of this leak and stop it at once.'

She looked at them again. Most of the

faces looked stunned, several who had been against the expansion wore a 'told-you-so' expression and a few looked uneasy. Geoffrey's face was dark with fury. Nigel Earnshaw was impassive, his eyes giving away nothing.

'You mean someone's been double-crossing us?' He sounded like an old American movie. 'Who? Who is it?'

'That's what we have to find out.' Felicity was careful not to look at Nigel now. She had decided not to voice her own suspicions until the Board had thoroughly discussed the matter and perhaps come to the same conclusion. 'And it shouldn't be too difficult. It has to be someone who knew about that project in detail. Someone with access to the files, someone who could be seen referring to them without arousing suspicion.'

'That only applies to a few of us,' one of the women members said, speaking for the first time. Felicity nodded.

'I'm afraid it does.'

'But it doesn't have to be a Board member!' Geoffrey was outraged. 'We're not the only ones with that kind of access. What about your secretary, Jackie Brent? Or one of the others? They must be equally aware of what can be done with information.'

'I don't believe it was any of them,' Felicity said slowly. 'The implications are too wide. Besides, if it were a secretary she'd know it would mean the loss of her job – and would she be able to count on whoever bought us out to employ her? Knowing what she was?'

'Hm.' Geoffrey looked unconvinced. 'Well, I still think they ought to be investigated. Anyone with access to the offices involved. That's primarily yours, Felicity.'

'And yours,' she reminded him. 'And ... Nigel's.'

'I hope you're not accusing either of us,' he said, bristling like a large dog scenting cats on his territory.

'I'm not accusing anyone at the moment. I'm merely clarifying what you said yourself.'

Nigel Earnshaw leaned forward a little. His voice, slightly harsh, had always grated a little on Felicity's nerves. It grated even more now.

'Felicity's right, you know, Geoff,' he said. 'The files have been more in our offices than anywhere else, and we've discussed the matter between us a great deal. If there is a leak–'

'There's no doubt about that, I'm afraid,'

Felicity told him.

'—then we ought at least to investigate our own offices before we start looking at anyone else. See if we can find out how it could have happened – without one of the three of us being directly involved.'

Felicity looked at him with grudging admiration. How devious could you get! He had made no hasty, guilt-betraying denials, shown no indignation at the hint of suspicion attaching itself to him, even proposed that his office should be investigated along with herself and Geoffrey. And at the same time, managed to convey the suggestion that the leak might be nothing to do with any of them but a matter of mismanagement rather than blatant espionage.

She had no doubt that he had covered his tracks well. When the leak was discovered to have emanated from his office, as she was certain it would be, there would be nothing that would enable them to accuse him directly. Meanwhile, his plans would continue to go through and Felicity would be helpless to prevent the ruin of all that she had built up.

'Why don't we three get together – with the approval of the rest of the Board, of course,' Nigel went on smoothly, 'and conduct our own preliminary investigation. There needn't be any fear of a cover-up. Two of us, presumably, are innocent and anxious to discover the truth. And it would permit the rest of the Board to continue with their own important work.'

'That makes sense,' said a voice, as Felicity hesitated, and several others agreed.

'Well, all right, if everyone agrees with that?' She glanced round and saw that most of the members were only too pleased to allow the unpleasant task to be carried out by someone else. 'In that case, Nigel, Geoffrey, we'd better start straightaway. We'll go to my office first. I'll tell Jackie we're not to be disturbed.'

She led the way out of the boardroom, thinking again how chilly and unwelcoming a room it was and remembering the day when she had shown it to Jake and he'd shared her feelings about it. They seemed to share so much now, and yet on that first day he had done nothing but exasperate her. She remembered asking him why he had taken up painting as a career, unable to believe that anyone could find satisfaction in such a dilettante pursuit.

She thought of him now, in his sunny garden, sketching the birds and butterflies that surrounded him, producing things of beauty with his own hands. Using the talent he had been born with to make the world a better place tending his own patch.

In her office, she faced the two men and sighed.

'Well, we'd better get this over with. I might as well tell you that I have a very good idea who is betraying the company. And I'm very sorry to have to say that, even to think it. But there's no other explanation. Sir Michael–'

'Just a moment,' Geoffrey interrupted. 'Just what makes you so certain there's no other explanation? What makes you think we three are the only people who could possibly have given this information away?'

Felicity stared at him. 'Why, that's obvious, surely. We're the only ones who have it, or have had access to it. Nobody else could have had the opportunity to study the files – they've always been kept under lock and key when one or another of us wasn't working on them. And we've had meetings and discussions between the three of us. I don't see what you're driving at.'

'Don't you?' Geoffrey's pale eyes fixed on her. 'Are you sure of that, Felicity? Can you really not think of anyone else who might have had the chance of looking at those papers, of overhearing our discussions?'

'No, I can't! There's never been anyone–' She looked at his face, caught the expression in his eyes and, with a sudden flash of pain, knew just what he was driving at. 'No,' she whispered. *'No.'*

'Yes,' he said firmly. 'Ashton. He was in and out of your office, and mostly in, during the whole period when those negotiations were at their most crucial. He could have overheard anything. He had ample opportunity to look at those papers. And even when he wasn't in here, he was wandering loose around the place. Butting in on us all, pretending to be getting "atmosphere". Atmosphere! I never trusted him, never, and now look where he's landed us.'

'I did warn you about the possibility,' Nigel said to her, quietly.

Felicity stared from one to the other. The thought that it could be Jake who had betrayed them hit her like a physical blow. Everything that was in her rebelled against any such possibility. 'He'd never do such a thing,' she said. 'Never.'

'And how can you be so sure of that?' Geoffrey sneered. 'What do you know of him, after all? Oh, we all know the man's got you dazzled with his artistic charm – half the women in the place seem to be falling over themselves to get him to notice them, God knows why! But what's he really up to? All that insistence on spending time with each Board member, sitting in each office, nicely placed to hear any phone calls, listening in on meetings on the pretext of being able to observe us together. Didn't any of that strike you as being distinctly overdone? And didn't it strike you as being a trifle suspicious that of all the offices he spent time in, he spent longest of all in yours?'

'But that was merely because I'm the Managing Director,' Felicity protested. 'Geoff, you're wrong about this, I know it. And I'll tell you why. Because the final figures, the ones that Sir Michael showed me, weren't agreed until after Jake had stopped sitting in here. He couldn't have seen them.'

'Whoever leaked this information,' Geoffrey said, 'must have been in your office the day you got that call to go to your father. If you remember, I'd brought you those new figures only that afternoon. Ashton was here then. He was with you when the call came through. You told me that yourself.'

Felicity's heart sank. She looked at Geoffrey, then at Nigel. She remembered her panic as Peggy had told her the news about her father, her haste to drop everything and go to him as quickly as possible. She remembered Jake, offering to put away the papers that were on her desk. The papers Geoffrey had brought her a few hours earlier. He had even told her he knew how to work the safe, simply from watching her do it so many times.

The eyes of both men were on her. She dropped her gaze, stared unseeingly at the polished wood of her desk.

'You can't deny he had the opportunity,' Geoffrey persisted. 'And you owe it to us all to investigate him first.' He stood up, looking down at her. 'He's the stranger in the house, Felicity. He might have got you dazzled, but until he came there was never any suggestion of a leak. And I'd like it put on record now that I'll have no further hand in any investigation until Ashton has been thoroughly questioned. I'll do it myself, if necessary.'

'No!' Felicity's reaction was betrayingly quick. She felt the colour wash over her face as she looked first at Geoffrey, then at Nigel. 'I'll go and see him myself. It's all right. You don't have to worry, I shan't be dazzled, as you call it. I mean to find out the truth about this, whoever turns out to be at the bottom of it.'

Geoffrey looked dissatisfied and started to speak, but Nigel Earnshaw held up a thin hand. 'I think we should let Felicity do this,' he said quietly. 'We've been forewarned – it's only fair that Ashton should be as well. We can carry out any formal investigation later, as formally as you like.'

Felicity looked at him in surprise. Convinced as she was that he was the guilty one, she wondered what could possibly be behind his apparent support. Or was he even more clever and devious than she had thought?

But she didn't have time to consider that now. She stood up, her fingertips resting on her desk.

'Thank you, Nigel. I think it's best if I go at once, don't you? We need to clear this up as quickly as possible.'

'Go?' Geoffrey exclaimed. 'You mean you're going to his house? Felicity, that's ridiculous! Bring him here. Far better to see him on your own ground, and you'll have Nigel and me here to support you.'

And that's just what I don't want, she

thought, and knew with a shock of dismay that she wasn't as convinced as she wanted to be about Jake's innocence. After all, he had been here at all the right times. He had had the opportunity...

Jake, her heart cried. Jake, no. I won't believe it ... I won't...

'Well, hello, Felicity. This is a nice surprise, in the middle of the day.' Jake stepped aside, beckoning her into the cool kitchen. His eyes were bright and questioning. 'There must be a very special reason for you to tear yourself away from your work to come and see me.'

'There is. Can we go into the other room, Jake?'

'Certainly.' He ducked under the low beam. 'You sound very serious. Care for a coffee? Or a cold drink?'

'No, thank you.' She stood indecisively in the middle of the room, her eyes roving over the cheerful untidiness without really seeing it. 'Well, a cold one, please. It's hotter than ever today.'

'Hate to say it, but we really need rain. Everything's getting very dry.' He disappeared into the kitchen and she heard the chink of glass. Unable to stand still, she moved over to the easel and looked at the canvas there.

'You've started on the picture, I see,' she said as Jake came back with a tray on which stood a tall glass jug and two tumblers.

'Yes. You're not supposed to be looking at it yet.' She heard the tinkle of ice as he poured from the jug. 'There you are, fresh lemonade made by my own fair hand. I'm thinking of joining the Women's Institute, did I tell you? My blackcurrant jam is out of this world. Well, what d'you think of it?'

Felicity stared dully at the half-finished picture, then made an effort. 'It looks as if it will be very good. The grouping's very effective. Me at the desk, the others all around the room. It's got a lot of life.'

'Yes, well, I appreciate your remarks, if not your enthusiastic tone.' Jake took the glass from her hand, set it on a small table and turned her to face him. 'What is it, Felicity? What's happened to upset you? Is it your father?'

Felicity shook her head. She could not bring herself to meet his eyes. 'No, Dad's fine. It – it's something else. Something serious.'

'Yes, I can see that. All right. Sit down and tell me what it is.'

He guided her to a sofa and sat beside her, but when he moved to slip his arm around her shoulders Felicity moved away to an armchair. She caught the look of surprise on his face and her heart ached. She didn't believe what Geoffrey had suggested, but until she and Jake had talked it through, she dared not let him touch her.

'What's wrong, Felicity?' he asked quietly, watching her.

How was she to say this?

'Jake ... we've had some bad news at Stallymore. No, not Dad' – as he made a quick movement – 'it's a business matter. Sir Michael Butterford came to see me early this morning. He brought proof that someone's been working against us, releasing information that ought not to be released. He had figures that could only have been seen by three people at Stallymore – and possibly one other. I called a Board meeting straight away.' She met his eyes at last, her own wide, tormented pools of pain. 'Jake, those figures were on my desk the day Dad was taken ill. You – you said you'd put them in my safe.'

There was a stillness in the room. Even the birds outside seemed hushed. Jake sat quite still, his expression frozen, his body rigid.

Only his eyes betrayed a powerful reaction, somewhere deep inside him.

'I'm afraid you'll have to explain yourself a little more clearly than that,' he said at last, and reached for his drink. 'I don't know what you're talking about.'

Felicity gazed at him, miserably aware that she had expressed herself badly, that her words sounded almost like an accusation. But why hadn't he denied it at once? It was all she wanted to hear, his reassurance that he'd had nothing to do with it.

'Jake, I'm sorry, I have to ask this,' she floundered. 'Those papers – the figures – you could have seen them. You know Sir Michael, you have contacts in his company – his daughter – you could have done it, Jake. I don't believe it, but–'

'Don't you?' he asked dryly. 'Then why are you here?'

'Because Geoffrey and Nigel insisted you should be questioned, because I didn't want to ask you to come to Stallymore. Jake, just tell me–'

'Tell you what? That I didn't steal your precious figures? Or that I did?' His eyes glinted dangerously. 'What happened to trust, Felicity? Don't I have the right to expect any?'

251

'Of course you do! I told you, I didn't believe it. But you don't seem to believe me. You seem to think I'm accusing you–'

'It certainly sounds like it.'

'Then perhaps it's your own guilty conscience!' she flashed in exasperation, and stopped in horror. But the damage was done.

Jake gave her a long, measuring look. He lay back on the sofa and stared at the ceiling. Only a small muscle, twitching in his jaw, betrayed any emotion.

'I think you'd better explain to me just what I've done,' he said at last. 'I'm afraid I don't have your head for the business world. As I once told you, it's a closed book to me.'

He wasn't going to say it. He wasn't going to tell her it wasn't true. And she stared at him and felt the pain begin inside her, the pain of betrayal of the cruellest kind, forcing the bitter words from her.

'Not so closed that you didn't realise the value of the information that came your way while you were in my office,' she said. 'Jake, stop pretending. It's over. I may be able to persuade the Board not to take action against you. But–'

'Felicity,' he said, 'will you believe me, *I don't know what you're talking about*. And

252

how does Mike Butterford come into it? Look, you're going to have to explain properly. As far as I'm concerned, you're talking in riddles.'

'Oh, am I?' Anger began to take the place of the confusion of distress and disbelief that had been churning inside her. 'All right, listen to this. Important information about a certain contract has been reaching the wrong people. They've been able to use it for their own purposes, which could quite easily bring about the downfall of Grant Holdings. If we're not very careful and very lucky too, we may find ourselves being taken over by unscrupulous buyers who will strip us of all our assets and leave us to rot. Now, I thought at first that this leak was the work of a certain member of the Board, and I was even prepared to accuse him. But then I was presented with other evidence. Evidence that pointed to you.' The pain almost overwhelmed her again and she turned her head away, unable to go on.

'I see. And just what was this other evidence?'

Felicity looked sadly at him. 'It was the day Dad was taken ill. You were in my office when the call came through. You offered to put away my papers – and among them were the papers that had the final figures on them, the ones that were leaked. Nobody else had seen them.'

'Nobody at all?'

'Well, only Geoff Hall. He brought them in to me himself that afternoon. He–'

'And couldn't he,' Jake asked quietly, 'have been your mole? Your traitor?'

Felicity stared at him. Once again, all her conceptions had taken a nosedive, turned on their heads. She felt bemused, off-balance, as if the world had shifted under her feet and might do so again at any moment. She shook her head, trying to clear it, but the mist of perplexity still hung about her brain.

'Presumably he, as chief accountant, was privy to all these secrets?' Jake said. 'Maybe he had his eyes on your chair, Felicity. After all, if he could discredit you in some way ... the leak might just be a means to an end.'

Felicity thought of Geoffrey's attitude to her: the clumsy courtship and proposal, the veiled threats he had made. Had he been preparing to accuse her of the leak, or of simple incompetence, of an almost crim-inally casual treatment of the company's affairs? Had he really been prepared to tell the Board about the evening when he had found her and Jake together in her bath-room, his suspicions about that first weekend when she had visited her father? Was all this some deep, Machiavellian plan to oust her from her position so that he could step into her shoes?

'Just what do you want to prove, Felicity?' Jake asked quietly. 'That I'm some sort of scoundrel who's been spending the last few weeks spying on you? That that's why I wanted to spend so much time in your office with you? Instead of–'

He stopped abruptly, his face dark with emotion. Felicity watched him and her heart cried out in pain. What was happening – what were they doing to each other?

But she had to know.

'Instead of what, Jake?' she asked softly, and the eyes he turned on her then were pools of torment, dark with their own secrets.

'Instead of simply wanting to be with you,' he said at last. 'That's why I wanted to spend that time in your office, Felicity. Oh, I needed to be there to get to know you, that was true enough. But I could have done all I needed in a quarter of the time. I just wanted to make it last. I wanted to get to know you – I wanted *you* to get to know me.

It was the only way I could think of.' His mouth twisted. 'It never struck me that I might end up being branded as a spy.'

Felicity gasped and flung herself across the space between them. She caught at his shoulders, stared into his shuttered face, then placed her two hands one on each side of his head and dragged his face down to hers. It was the first kiss she had instigated, and she felt his lips quiver under hers, stiffen with resistance and then, slowly, begin to respond. As her own mouth relaxed against his, she felt the heat of desire wash over her, and her limbs grew weak as she melted against his body.

'Oh, Jake,' she whispered. 'I never believed it – I swear I didn't. But I had to ask... I made a mess of it. And you didn't help.'

'I couldn't,' he admitted, his arms tightly wound around her body. 'I was so shattered at the thought that you could be accusing me of industrial espionage. Me! Why, I wouldn't even know a microfiche if I caught it on a line!'

Felicity laughed in spite of herself. She lay against him, rejoicing in the rapture of knowing that everything was right between them again. Then her heart sank as she realised that nothing could be called all right until this sordid business was resolved.

'Geoff,' she said slowly. 'I think you're right, Jake. But I thought it was Nigel. I thought he was the one who wanted my job.'

'I'm sure a lot of men would like to have your job,' Jake said. 'But simply because you find them physically unattractive, it doesn't mean they're preparing to cut your throat to get it.'

Felicity blushed deeply. 'It's not just the way he looks,' she protested. 'I've never really liked him. He – he smokes a lot. And he's never been very friendly.'

'Both of which, of course, prove him to be a villain. Felicity' – Jake leaned forward – 'we don't all have to like each other. And just because our personalities clash, it doesn't mean those we dislike are necessarily crooks. As a matter of fact, I think your Nigel suffers from nothing much worse than shyness. He's good at his job and he gets on with that, but on a personal level he has difficulty. I should think the last thing he wants is your job.'

Felicity was silent for a moment, considering this. Then she looked up at him.

'I've accused you of some dreadful things,' she said in a low voice. 'Jake, I don't know what to say. I ought to have believed in you.'

'Yes, well, it would have been nice,' he said, draining his glass. 'But we can't have everything we want in this world. Although I did think we were working towards a kind of trust. Still, never mind. And you don't know that I'm right about Geoffrey, even now. I could be simply pulling the wool over your eyes.'

'Jake – what can I say?'

'Nothing, I think would be the best idea.' He got to his feet, reached for her hands and pulled her up against him. She stood quite still, feeling his body close, wanting nothing more at this moment than to rest against him, feel his lips on hers, his hands on her body ... to forget everything but the two of them, in their own world, far removed from that of big business.

'Go and finish your investigations,' he said gently. 'Find out the truth, and then make up your mind what to do about it. Then, if you want to, you can come back. But this time, Felicity, we're going to have to stop the games we've been playing until now. If you come back here again, it's got to be for real.'

She looked at him, understanding dimly that he was issuing some kind of ultimatum.

'Jake ... I don't know what you're asking

me to do.'

'I'm not asking you to do anything,' he said quietly. 'I've never been in the business of asking a woman to give up the career she loves for me. But I want you to understand yourself, your own motives for doing what you do. I want you to be quite certain of your own commitments. And I think you do understand, Felicity, in your heart. In that deep, secret heart that you haven't consulted yet.'

He turned her around and gave her a gentle push towards the door. Like a sleepwalker, Felicity allowed him to guide her through the tangled garden, with its kaleidoscope of colour, to the gate. He opened the door of her car and waited for her to slide in.

'You're sending me away, aren't you?'

'You know you have to go,' he said, and his face was unsmiling.

'Jake...' But she was in the car, the door closed upon her. In a daze, she turned the key and let the engine start. Her body functioning, it seemed, without the will of her mind, she put the car into gear and moved away down the lane.

The tears were hot on her cheeks as she drove back to Stallymore Castle, to face

259

Nigel Earnshaw and Geoffrey. It had to be done. She had brought herself to this position, through her own ambition, her own burning desire to succeed. And she knew that she would not fail, even now. Grant Holdings could still be saved.

But Grant Holdings no longer seemed very important. For the sake of the people who depended on the company for their livelihood, she knew that every effort must be made to save it – but it had lost its grip on her heart, dropped sharply from first place in her life.

That place now belonged at last to a man. To Jake Ashton. But she did not know if she would ever be able to convince him of this.

Ten

'So there it is,' Felicity said quietly, and looked at the two men who sat opposite her. 'I've seen Jake Ashton and he emphatically denies any connection with the leak. There seems to be only one conclusion to draw.'

'That he's lying,' Geoffrey said at once. Felicity looked at Nigel Earnshaw. He met her eyes steadily, his own expression un-readable.

'I don't think Jake's lying,' she said to Geoffrey.

'You don't mean you suspect Nigel here? Now, that's just plain daft! Why, he's one of the most loyal members we've got. And he didn't have a chance to see those figures.' Geoffrey turned suddenly to stare at the other man, his eyes narrowing. 'Or did you? All that week when Felicity was away, you were in and out of here a lot. Surely you didn't – I won't believe it.'

It was very well done, Felicity thought, watching him. In fact, she might almost have believed it herself, prejudiced against Nigel as she had been. She realised again just how unfair she had been to this man, how blind in her judgement. Just because she found him physically unappealing, just because she'd never taken the trouble to find out what lay behind the barriers he erected.

'No,' she said before Nigel could speak. 'I don't suspect Nigel. I don't believe he ever did see those figures. But you did, Geoffrey.'

Geoffrey swung back to stare at her. 'Well, of *course* I did! I brought them in to you myself. For God's sake, Felicity, you're not

261

seriously suggesting that I used my own knowledge–'

'Nobody knew more about it than you,' she said. 'Nobody was better placed.'

'But, look here,' he blustered, 'that's nothing short of ridiculous. I suppose you're saying that I spent the next week, while you were away, working behind your back, while Ashton never had an opportunity, of course. What about all those hours you spent at the hospital? He could have been doing anything!'

'In fact, he was in the hospital with me, either visiting Dad or sitting on the other side of the door. And when I wasn't in the hospital, we were going for walks or drives together. He hardly left my side, the whole of that week, Geoffrey. He never had any opportunity to pass information.'

'Not at night either?' Geoffrey sneered. 'I suppose we can take it for granted he had no opportunities then!'

'That's enough!' To Felicity's astonishment, Nigel Earnshaw spoke in sharp, angry tones. 'You've said more than enough. I've had just about as much as I can stand of your slimy tongue and filthy accusations. I've sat here and listened, but I'll listen no more. You'll hear what I have to say for a change.' He stood up, tall and cadaverous, his purplish eyes fixed on Geoffrey's face with bitter contempt. 'I've had my suspicions of you for a long time, Hall. You've been altogether too keen on making up to our Managing Director here, getting your foot in the door. Oh yes, I know about your cosy Friday afternoon tête-à-têtes and the little outings to the theatre or a restaurant that followed them. It was pretty plain what you were up to, but what could I or anyone else do about that? Felicity wouldn't look twice at me, and anything I might have said would have been put down to jealousy and spite. Well, she's a grown woman and ought to be able to look after herself, but–'

'I wish you wouldn't talk about me as if I weren't here,' Felicity said. Her face was burning. Had everyone been watching Geoffrey and herself, speculating about them?

Nigel glanced at her in apology. 'I'm sorry, Felicity. But it's been hard enough, all these months, having to stand by and watch this – this *toad* curry favour with you, knowing it was all for his own disgusting purposes. You don't know him–'

'And neither do you!' Geoffrey shouted,

leaping to his feet. 'And neither, I may say, do you know our esteemed MD. No! Shall I tell you what I found when I happened to call at her flat one evening? Only a quiet little game of mock bullfighting going on in her bathroom, that's all! Our Chairman here capering about in the buff, while Jake Ashton played the part of the dashing matador. Is that the kind of person you want to work for, Nigel? Don't you think we'd be better off under new management?'

'I certainly think *you* would be,' said a familiar voice, and they all turned in astonishment to see Jake Ashton himself at the door, with Jackie hovering apologetically behind him. 'It's all right, Jackie – Miss Grant won't blame you. Go back to your desk.' He strode into the room, slamming the door closed behind him, and cast a glance, half-humorous, half-rueful, at Felicity. 'I'm not as strong as I thought,' he said wryly. 'I thought I could wait until you saw your own way through this. But I guess my male ego's as big as the next man's. I had to come along and stick my oar in.'

'Oh, Jake,' Felicity said faintly. 'Thank goodness you're here.' Ignoring the other two, she ran round her desk and into his arms as if she were a ship running for shelter in a safe harbour.

He caught her and held her close for a few moments. Then, gently, he put her away from him and looked into her eyes.

'It's still your pigeon,' he said quietly. 'I can't sort this out for you. All I can do is give you my support.'

'I know, Jake, and it's all right. That's what I need.' She turned. back to the two men who stood watching. 'Well, Geoffrey? You know we can prove what you've been doing, don't you? Nobody could have known those figures or had the opportunity to pass them on, other than you. You're not going to deny it any more, are you?'

Geoffrey stared at her, his pale eyes prominent, shot with blood, and she shivered a little at the naked enmity they revealed. Had it always been there, that hatred? Could he really have hidden it so well? Could she really have been so blind to the truth?

'It would have happened sooner or later, anyway,' he muttered. 'You were never really up to this job, Felicity. Oh, you did well enough, I grant you, but you always relied far too much on your Board. You always trusted people too much, and you can't afford that in this world.'

Felicity was saddened by the indictment, but she faced the fact that it was probably true. She had always trusted those she worked with – and, as Geoffrey had proved, it had been a mistake.

'I'd like you to go and get your personal possessions out of your office, Geoffrey,' she said. 'Nigel will go with you, won't you, Nigel? And then we'll have to discuss what action to take over this. It may take a little time – I'll need to call another Board meeting. We'll let you know as soon as our decision is reached. Meanwhile, I take it you'll be letting us have your formal resignation.'

Geoffrey opened his mouth to argue, then closed it again. He looked like nothing so much as a large, stranded fish gasping for air. Jake would have to change his cartoon representation, Felicity thought, but the idea brought her little amusement. She watched the two men leave the room and then turned to Jake.

'Thank you for coming,' she said simply, and lifted her face as he came to take her in his arms.

'That isn't the end of it though, is it?' he said after the kiss. 'You still have a lot of thinking to do, Felicity – a lot of decisions to come to.'

'I know,' she said. 'And I want you to come with me while I do my thinking.'

She went to the door and through to the outer office where Jackie was sitting at her desk, trying to look as if she were working but failing. The secretary looked up as Felicity appeared, and her eyes were bewildered.

'What's happening, Miss Grant? The other Board members keep ringing, wanting to talk to you, and Mr Hall and Mr Earnshaw went through here just now looking like thunder. And I'm sorry about Mr Ashton, but he wouldn't take no for an answer, he just stormed straight past me–'

'It's all right, Jackie. Everything's under control. And it doesn't matter about Mr Ashton. As it happens, we're just going out together, for a walk.'

'A *walk*?' The secretary's eyes seemed to be in danger of falling out of her head entirely. 'But, Miss Grant, you've got that meeting with Miss Exton in half an hour, and–'

'Tell Miss Exton it's postponed until tomorrow. And cancel all the rest of my appointments for today. Oh, and get the Board together first thing tomorrow for a special meeting, will you? That's all except Mr Hall – he's resigned.'

'*Resigned?*' Jackie blinked. 'But–'

'It'll all be explained later,' Felicity said. 'And it's not a pleasant story, so I'd be grateful if you'd discourage any gossip among the rest of the staff. Everyone will know all they need to know quite soon. Now I'm going out.'

Jackie stared at her, then at Jake. As Felicity reached the door, she turned back in time to see a huge wink close one of Jake's eyes. The secretary's bemused expression collapsed into a giggle.

'You!' Felicity said to him as they went down the stairs and stepped outside into the sunshine. 'You're absolutely impossible.'

'I've told you before, I'm not at all impossible,' he said meekly. 'Just a little unlikely. Please, where are we going?'

'I told you. For a walk.' At a brisk pace, she crossed the smooth lawn, passing the brilliant display of roses, and made for the trees that edged the lawn. Jake, silent for once, followed her. Together, they passed into the shadowy wood.

'I haven't been here for years,' Felicity said quietly as she led the way along the tiny, criss-crossing paths. 'It doesn't seem to have changed at all.'

'Tell me about when you came before.'

'I was on my own,' she said, thinking of the first time she had penetrated here, uncertain, enjoyably half-scared, imagining herself to be in the Wild Wood with Kenneth Grahame's sinister whistling creatures all around her. 'I'd been reading *Wind in the Willows*. I used to practically live the books I read in those days.'

'I wonder you weren't terrified. That's a pretty scary passage, where Mole gets trapped by the weasels.'

'I think I was scared, but that was all part of it. And I didn't want to go back. For some reason or other, I was fed up with the rest of the children and wanted to show them I could do something on my own. I was something of a loner, even then,' she said wryly. 'Anyway, I went on and on along these tiny paths, convinced they would lead me to some magic place – I was into C. S. Lewis and Narnia by then, too. And suddenly–' She stopped and caught her breath. 'Suddenly, I was here, at this very spot.' Her voice was low, almost awed, and Jake came silently to stand beside her. He slipped an arm round her shoulders.

They were standing at the edge of a clearing. Around them, tall beech trees with trunks as grey as elephants' legs cast a shimmering green canopy over a burnished floor. Above the clearing, the sky shone clear and blue, reflected in the pool that lay at their feet.

'The Wood Between the Worlds,' Felicity said with a little laugh. 'I told you, I didn't know whether I was in *Wind in the Willows* or Narnia. Whichever it was, to me it was magic.'

'And what,' Jake said after a moment, 'did you do then?'

She blushed a little and smiled. 'It was a hot day. I was seven years old, quite un-inhibited, and I could swim like a fish. I took off all my clothes and went in.'

'Seems like a good idea,' he said. 'Why don't you repeat the experience?'

Felicity gave him a startled glance. 'Jake, don't be silly! Now? Anyone might come along and see. You–' She felt herself colour again.

'I've seen you naked before,' he reminded her. 'More than once, in fact.' He laughed at her expression. 'It's all right, I haven't been playing the peeping Tom and lurking round your bedroom window. But there was some-one else here that day, wasn't there? Someone who saw you then, swimming like a miniature mermaid? Or maybe you don't remember.'

'Yes.' Felicity stared at him. 'Yes, I remember. I remember very well. It was a boy. A boy of about sixteen. He swam with me. I never knew where he came from – he was just there, in the water, laughing at me. Afterwards we sat in the sun on that bank to dry off, and we talked. About books and birds and animals.' Her eyes had a faraway look in them, a look of memories brought back. 'Then he disappeared – I never saw him again. And I never knew his name... It was as if he wasn't quite real, he was just part of the magic of the place.' She turned and stared up at Jake, her eyes wondering. 'He said we would come here again and meet, one day,' she whispered. 'But he never came.'

'Didn't he?' Jake said softly. 'Are you sure?'

Felicity met his eyes. 'Not until today,' she said.

Slowly, he took her in his arms. She lifted her lips to his and felt a surge of joy as he began yet again the exploration that was still so new, yet so familiar. His hands moved over her body with sureness, touching, caressing, tender and firm, and his lips left hers to trace a path down the arching column of her throat, deep into the cleft between her breasts. His hands supported her as she trembled and softened against him, and he lowered her very gently to the ground and lay with her on the soft, springing grass.

'Why did you never come back here until today?' he asked. 'You've been at Stallymore for over a year now. Why did it take you so long?'

'I was afraid,' she said honestly. 'It's been a kind of talisman to me, this place. An idea of tranquillity, of magic, that I carried in my heart always. A sort of symbol of what life was all about – a secret I could never quite grasp. I didn't want to come back and find it was just a childish dream; no more than a rather muddy puddle in the middle of a few trees.'

'And didn't you want to meet your magic boy again?'

'I didn't think he would ever come back,' she said soberly. 'I thought I'd lost him for good. I've never found anyone else, Jake.'

'And I've never found anyone to take the place of my little mermaid. You stayed in my heart all those years, Felicity. When I heard you'd come back to Stallymore, I couldn't believe it. I came here at once. I kept coming. And then I saw what you'd done to the gardens and I knew you would never come.'

'The gardens?'

'You took away my wilderness,' he said. 'I did half those paintings you saw in these gardens.'

'And I didn't even share them with other people,' she said remorsefully. 'You were right, Jake – they were planned as no more than a setting, just like the rest of Stallymore. A stage set for the production I was so busy laying on – Felicity Grant in the hit of the season, Grant Industrial Holdings. Without people to enjoy them, they're empty, sterile.' She spoke with sudden decision. 'Well, I'm going to change that. I'm going to open Stallymore to the public – let them wander in the gardens, explore the woods, see the Great Hall and the old keep. It won't make any difference to the work that goes on there; we can keep the offices quite separate. And at least a few people about the place will stop it looking quite so dreadfully tidy.'

'That's my girl!' he said approvingly. 'Any other great ideas?'

'Yes.' She looked at him gravely. 'I'm going

to resign my position as Chairman and Managing Director.'

Jake stared at her. 'Felicity–'

'Not immediately,' she interrupted. 'That would look too strange, coming on top of Geoffrey's resignation. It's going to be hard enough stopping the rumours as it is. In a few months, a year, whenever the time seems right. I'm not tough enough for business, Jake. I've been lucky until now, I've never had to face real opposition. But this situation has shown me, and I don't want to be mixed up with that again. I'm beginning to think it was never right for me anyway – not for the real Felicity.'

'And which is the real Felicity and which the false?'

'The false Felicity,' she said slowly, 'is a girl who lost her way. Who was afraid of real emotion and pushed it away, out of sight; a girl who saw business as a safe place, somewhere where she could use any talents she possessed without ever getting really involved with people. That Felicity almost killed the real one, who wanted to get out and love and be loved, who wanted to run down to a pool on a hot day and swim naked and not care who saw her, who wanted to play at bullfighting in the bathroom, without someone thinking she was depraved. Who wanted – wants – to live among wild flowers and birds and butter-flies and think about the real world, rather than the artificial one we've concocted for ourselves.' She looked up at him with eyes that reflected the shimmering colour of the water. 'I am still that Felicity, aren't I?' she asked tremulously. 'It isn't too late, is it?'

'No,' Jake said, drawing her close against him, 'it isn't too late.'

Slowly, he began to kiss her again, his mouth exploring hers and then going on, with tantalising deliberation, to trace a path of tingling fire to her ears, her eyelids, and again down the throbbing pulses of her neck. His fingers pulled aside the collar of her shirt and slid the buttons from their moorings so that the soft silk drifted away, leaving her breasts hidden only by a wisp of lace. He found the front fastening of her bra and smoothed it aside, and then bent to lay his lips on the pale curves.

Felicity lay quiescent in his arms, trembling like a fawn, no longer trying to quieten the thundering of her heart. She felt his mouth against her throbbing skin and twisted beneath him, moaning softly, arching herself towards him. He lifted his head to hers again and she clasped him against her, opening her mouth to his, her fingers tangled in his thick, dark hair, her body driven by a desire she scarcely recognised but knew must at all costs be satisfied. An urgency she had never experienced before swept through her shuddering body and she lifted herself in his arms, straining against him, whimpering with frantic need.

'Ssh ... ssh ... not too fast, my darling.' Jake pulled slightly away and leaned over her, his eyes as dark as the pool on a stormy day. 'If this is going to happen now,' he murmured, 'we must keep it under control, not let it take charge.' He traced one finger down her cheek, letting it rove down to her breast and make tiny circles there. 'Not, at least, until a good while later ... I don't want this to be over in five minutes.'

Felicity gazed up at him, then relaxed in his arms. The grass was a soft bed beneath her, the trees a shifting canopy above. The sun filtered down through their moving pattern of leaves in a sheen of silver and blue seen through a filigree of palest green. Around them, there was no sound but the singing of birds high in the branches, the rustling of those who were busy going to and fro to feed nestlings.

Slowly, with delicate movements, Jake began to remove the rest of Felicity's clothes. His fingertips brushed her body lightly, intimately, lingering here and there until she was driven almost to frenzy. She lay beneath his tender scrutiny, yearning for his touch again, then lifted her hands to his body and tugged at his own shirt, at the waistband of his jeans, baring him to her gaze and remembering the slender boy of over twenty years ago, seeing him merge and blend with this mature body, with a full and undeniable masculinity that sprang to her touch.

'Didn't I always say there was a real woman in there, a wild creature that nobody had ever tamed?' Jake breathed, and he quivered as he laid his body on hers and both cried out at the fiery contact of skin against skin.

'And are you going to tame me?' she whispered against his lips, and felt him shake his head.

'Never.' The word was spoken straight into her throat. 'Never. I believe in wild animals staying wild ... oh, Felicity, *Felicity*...'

He seemed to have forgotten about keeping their desire under control. Instead, his fingers were hard as they gripped her, his arms like iron bands. His legs were taut as they twined with hers, and as she ran her hands down the length of his body she could feel each muscle rigidly outlined. A brief tremor of fear shook her as she realised that this man was now in the grip of a passion to which there could be only one end. Then she was as lost as he, swept headlong by a desire that took them like a tropical storm, thundering in their ears, crashing about their bodies, raging around them as they reached deep into each other's souls to attain a final, brilliant flash of consummation that left them both breathless, awash in each other's arms.

'I don't need to ask any more questions, do I?' he murmured after a long time into the hollow of her neck. 'You've answered them all ... oh, Felicity, my darling, my sweet. I've waited a long time for you to come back to me.'

'You couldn't have fallen in love with me then,' she protested. 'Not when I was seven.'

'No? Why do you think I never came back? I knew it was crazy – a sixteen-year-old boy and a child of seven. It scared me so much that I kept clear of this wood and of you and your cousins for the rest of that holiday. It was only later that I got to know Andrew, when you'd stopped coming. I kept track of you through him, hoping that we'd meet again some day, but when I heard how successful a businesswoman you'd become I thought I'd lost you. I thought my mermaid girl had gone for ever.'

'Well, as you see, she hadn't.' Felicity twisted herself gently out of his arms and stood up, still glowing from his loving, on the edge of the pool. 'Is it deep enough to swim in, I wonder? Oh, yes – and it's deliciously cold!'

She slipped into the water, feeling it like silk against her burning skin, and swam across the pool, her strokes sending up a bright spray of water. At the far side, she turned on her back and looked for Jake. And saw him, tall and bronzed, as splendid as a Greek statue in his nakedness, poised on the bank for a moment before he dived in.

He surfaced beside her, shaking back his glinting hair, laughing and reaching for her, but instantly she turned in the water, twisted under his arm and swam back beneath the surface to the bank where they had made love. She hauled herself out and sat there, smiling, as he emerged to sit beside her.

'I hope I was right in thinking nobody ever comes here,' she remarked. 'It would be slightly embarrassing if half the office staff were to troop down here with their lunch-time sandwiches and find us disporting ourselves.'

'Does that matter?' he asked. 'If you're going to give up your position? Felicity, did you mean that? You've not had much time to think about it – I wouldn't want you to do anything hasty.'

She shook her head. 'I won't be. I've had it in my mind for a long time, without being properly aware of it. This morning, I saw it as the only answer for me. I don't want that life any more, Jake. It's like that living room of mine – bare, sterile and unreal, all image and show. I'll still keep a connection with Grant Industrial Holdings and Stallymore, but I won't be running it any more.'

'And who will?'

'I think Nigel,' she said after a moment. 'I was quite wrong about him, Jake. I misread nearly everything he said and did. I could see he was brilliant at his job, but I never bothered to find out any more about him. You know, he as good as told me he'd been in love with me for months – and all the time, I was suspecting him of trying to steal my job. Well, he can have it now, and welcome – if he wants it.'

'I've already told you, I don't think he will. You'd do a lot better to give him Geoffrey's job, if he's qualified to do it. Why not consider one of the women? They seemed rather bright to me. And it would carry on a fine tradition.'

Felicity smiled. 'You are an old charmer, Jake Ashton,' she said softly. 'And you think your charm will get you anywhere you want to be, don't you?'

'I hope so,' he murmured, taking her in his arms again and sliding one hand down to her thighs. 'I certainly hope so ... Felicity, we are going to be married, aren't we? You will come to live with me in my wilderness?'

'Just as soon as I can,' she whispered as she settled back against his warm, pulsing body. 'Just as soon as I can...'

'And so this is the picture that caused all the trouble.' John Grant looked up at the wall of Felicity's office and nodded slowly. 'A fine piece of work. You can be proud of that, Jake.'

'I'm not displeased with it,' Jake said gravely. The four of them examined the painting, seeing how Jake had captured the gentle glow of the wood panelling, the translucent quality of the light that came softly through the windows, the colours of the Turkish carpet that covered the floor. But all that was merely the background. Bringing the picture vibrantly to life were the figures it portrayed: Felicity at her desk, small and yet plainly in command; the rest of the Board around her, all turned slightly to look towards her – Nigel, Andrew and the others – all except Geoffrey, whose absence did not even leave a gap.

'Yes. A very fine picture.' John Grant turned away and walked over to the window. He was thinner than before his heart attack, more finely drawn, but otherwise looked as fit as he had before it happened. He looked down at the gardens, once again with roses in bloom, but no longer empty. Instead, there were people down there, walking along the paths, admiring the flowers, sitting on the seats to chat and enjoy the brilliant warmth of the sun.

'I like Stallymore like this,' he said, turning back. 'And I like to see you happy too, Felicity. You're looking more beautiful than ever. Don't you agree, my dear?'

His wife smiled and nodded. Peggy and John Grant had been married soon after

Jake and Felicity. They had spent the past few months on a cruise and only recently returned to visit Felicity on her last day at Stallymore Castle.

'Now you're to look after yourself,' John Grant said. 'No more worries about business, understand? I don't want my grandchild to come into the world with a financial statement clutched in his hand.'

'He won't.' Felicity, no longer slender, moved into the circle of her husband's arm. 'And now you've seen the picture, you're to come to the farewell lunch in the Great Hall. And after that we're all going back to the cottage.'

'That's right,' Jake said. 'There's a lot of work to be done there. We've got to get it ready for the rest of the bargain.'

'The rest of the bargain? I don't understand.'

'Well, we've started the first of the kids,' Jake said with the grin that had so exasperated Felicity when she had first met him. 'Now we've got to get on with the dogs, and the muddy footprints.'

The publishers hope that this book has given you enjoyable reading. Large Print Books are especially designed to be as easy to see and hold as possible. If you wish a complete list of our books please ask at your local library or write directly to:

Magna Large Print Books
Magna House, Long Preston,
Skipton, North Yorkshire.
BD23 4ND

This Large Print Book for the partially sighted, who cannot read normal print, is published under the auspices of

THE ULVERSCROFT FOUNDATION